"Cancel the wedding now."

Nick struggled to leash the ruthless passion that clamored through every cell in his body, urging him to pick her up and carry her into the bedroom and there lay claim to her. "Cat, you can't marry Glen," he said steadily, pouring his considerable power to persuade into his deep voice. "Cancel the wedding—I'll help you with the arrangements. It will be difficult, but we'll cope."

He almost had her. He could feel her hunger, feel her urge to surrender. She closed her eyes; when her lashes lifted the blue irises were smooth and opaque as enamel. "I don't know what this—thing—is between us, but it can't mean anything, because I don't know you. I do know Glen, and I not only love him, I respect him."

His demons unleashed by three sleepless nights and intense, aching frustration, Nick kissed her startled mouth.

D0829432

Passion™

in

Harlequin Presents®

Looking for sophisticated stories that **sizzle?**
Wanting a read that has a little extra **spice?**

Pick up a Presents *Passion*™ novel—
where **seduction** is *guaranteed!*

If you loved *A Ruthless Passion*,
you can read all about **Morna's** story
in Robyn Donald's follow-up:

The Temptress of Tarika Bay #2336

Coming next month from Harlequin Presents®

Robyn Donald

A RUTHLESS PASSION

Passion™

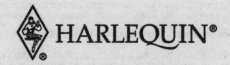

HARLEQUIN®

TORONTO • NEW YORK • LONDON
AMSTERDAM • PARIS • SYDNEY • HAMBURG
STOCKHOLM • ATHENS • TOKYO • MILAN • MADRID
PRAGUE • WARSAW • BUDAPEST • AUCKLAND

ISBN 0-373-12330-2

A RUTHLESS PASSION

First North American Publication 2003.

Visit us at www.eHarlequin.com

Printed in U.S.A.

PROLOGUE

NICK waited in the foyer of the hotel until Glen and Mrs Courtald had left for their appointment with the lawyer. He despised subterfuge, but what he had to say to Cat was too important to risk any interruption—especially not from her mother or fiancé.

When he knocked on the suite door he noted with an odd remoteness that his pulse-rate was up. And when he heard her call, 'Coming,' in the low, husky voice she'd grow into when she'd learned what sex was all about, his gut clenched and a charge of male hunger hit him with the force of a bomb.

The door opened. Cat's smoky blue eyes widened; colour surged through her exquisite skin before draining away. Her fingers tightened on the veil she'd been trying on—short and fluffy as befitted an eighteen-year-old bride.

'N-Nick,' she said unevenly. 'This is a surprise.'

'Ask me in,' he said tersely.

She hesitated, then stepped back. 'You've missed Glen—he and my mother have just gone.'

'I didn't come to see them,' he said, walking into the suite Glen had reserved for the girl he was marrying the following day—the best hotel in Auckland, as befitted the bride of one of New Zealand's top advertising men.

Its impersonal opulence should have overshadowed such a small person, yet in spite of her youth and her fragility Cat stood very erect, the ridiculous veil still perched on hair the polished red-brown of a chestnut, and although he

sensed her unease, her gaze was direct and steady. 'What
do you want?' she asked quietly.

Nick had had erotic dreams about that hair, and her slender body, and that ripe mouth, still innocent in spite of her
engagement to his friend. Glen was being very careful with
her, apparently content to wait until they were married before consummating their relationship.

Clamping down on a bitter, raw jealousy that astonished
and infuriated him, Nick said bluntly, 'Have you thought
what marriage to Glen will involve?'

'I might be only eighteen,' she returned with a cool dignity he found both maddening and provocative, 'but I'm
not a total idiot. Yes, I know what marriage involves. I
watch television, read newspapers and magazines and
books, go to films, talk to people.' She paused before adding with delicate sarcasm, 'And my parents were married.'

Did she know that his hadn't been? Possibly; Glen might
have told her. 'What people have you talked to? The pupils
at that expensive boarding school you graduated from at
the end of last year? What do they know?'

With a spark of temper she retorted, 'As much as any
kid who grows up on the streets, actually. Just because they
come from a different socio-economic group doesn't mean
that the same problems don't affect them.' Small face hot
with dismay, she went on swiftly, 'I'm sorry—I didn't
mean that you—'

'It doesn't matter,' he interrupted. 'I did grow up on the
streets, but I'm talking about the realities of life as a very
rich man's trophy wife.'

Her cheeks stung as though he'd hit them. 'I thought a
trophy wife was someone who took the place of the real
wife. Glen hasn't dumped anyone for me.'

Nick bit back his first, lethal response. It was no use
dragging in Morna's private tragedy; besides, technically

Cat was correct. Glen had never offered to marry the woman who'd been his lover for the past five years.

Instead, he said relentlessly, 'Glen is going to expect you to run his house, to plan dinners, to organise parties, to meet and charm clients. Can you do that?'

'I can try,' she said, adding on a note of uncertainty that wrung his heart, 'My mother will help me.'

'Your mother is not well.'

A shadow darkened her features. How much pressure, Nick wondered savagely, had Cat's charming, gentle, uncomplaining mother applied? Oh, nothing overt, but with her father dead, and his small annuity gone with him, Mrs Courtald must have seen Glen as the answer to all her prayers.

Cat said, 'She's—well enough.' Her full, soft mouth, tantalisingly red, tightened. 'And I'm a quick learner,' she finished on a challenging note.

She was going to go through with it. For only the second time in his life Nick braced himself as a shaft of panic overturned the processes of his cool, incisive brain. Reasserting control, he asked with cutting scorn, 'Why are you marrying him, Cat? If it's money—'

'It is *not* money!' Indignation woke those sleepy eyes to fiery alertness, jutted the small, pointed chin. Coldly she retorted, 'Glen's an attractive, exciting man, kind and thoughtful and fun to be with—'

'And twenty years older than you.'

Her chin jutted even further. 'So? I like older men.'

'Because you want a father to replace the one you've just lost,' he said brutally; he was doing this all wrong and he didn't know how to rescue the situation. 'But Glen is not yet forty, and he's no father figure. He's going to want to sleep with you, Cat—'

'Don't call me that!'

'Why not? You're like a cat, sweet and kittenish when everything's going your way, but I can see the feline in you. Glen can't—he thinks you're docile and obedient and playful. He's a virile man, experienced and vigorous. Have you thought of what it will be like to make love to him?'

Once again the colour drained from her face. Her lashes fell as she said angrily, 'I'm going to be the best wife I can possibly be to him—'

'Even though you want me?' Nick demanded.

Head down, face averted, she was shaking her head, the folds of tulle swinging in soft waves. 'No,' she said fiercely. 'I love Glen.'

'But you want me,' Nick repeated, sliding his hand beneath her chin, lifting her face. Mouth trembling, she looked at him with desolate, hungry eyes.

'Cancel the wedding now,' he pressed quietly, struggling to leash the ruthless passion that clamoured through every cell in his body, urging him to pick her up and carry her into the bedroom and there lay claim to her in the most primitive, effective way, stamp her with his possession, make her shrink with horror at the thought of any other man touching her. 'Cat, you can't marry Glen,' he said steadily, pouring his considerable power to persuade into his deep voice, into his expression. 'Cancel the wedding— I'll help you with the arrangements. It will be difficult, but we'll cope.'

He almost had her. He could feel her hunger, feel her urge to surrender—until her lashes dropped and her mouth tightened, and she said, 'And then what, Nick?'

His hand dropped to his side. 'I can help you,' he repeated, knowing as he said it that she wasn't going to give in on such a vague promise—and angry because he could offer her nothing more. Glen might be prepared to take advantage of a girl straight from school, but Nick knew she wasn't ready for marriage to anyone, much less the passion that hardened his body the moment he touched her.

She closed her eyes; when her lashes lifted the blue irises were smooth and opaque as enamel. 'I don't know what this—thing—is between us, but it can't mean anything because I don't know you. We only met three days ago. I do know Glen, and I not only love him, I respect him. I couldn't put him through the pain of such a public humiliation because of something that I don't understand and don't trust.' She looked at Nick directly. 'I'd have thought that as his closest friend and his protégé, you'd be ashamed even to suggest it.'

His demons unleashed by three sleepless nights and an intense, aching frustration, Nick kissed her startled mouth, forcing it open. Her scent, sweet and womanly, filled his head with narcotic fumes; he tried to drop his arms, lift his head and step back, but he couldn't move, overthrown by a ferocious, dangerous pleasure.

She didn't resist; after a few rigid seconds she yielded, her body sinking against his, her mouth softening beneath his.

So this, he thought dimly, was paradise...

When she stiffened and tried to push him away he let her go, only then aware that somebody was knocking on the door.

Huge, shamed eyes slid away from his. Cat pressed her hand against her mouth, then with sudden, deliberate violence wiped his kiss off. 'Get out,' she whispered. 'Just get out of here, and never come back. I wouldn't marry you if you were the last man in the world.'

Nick leaned over and straightened the crushed tulle of her veil. Amazingly his hands remained gentle, although he'd never felt so much like smashing everything in his life to bits.

'I don't remember offering you marriage. Think of that kiss when you're in bed with Glen,' he said savagely, and turned and walked out, striding without a backward look past the hotel maid who waited there.

CHAPTER ONE

Six years later

CAT stopped at the busy crossing, staring apprehensively at the building on the other side of the road. In the quick intimacy of a crowd, the man beside her followed her gaze.

'Magnificent, isn't it?' he observed chattily, his admiring gaze returning to Cat's small, fine-featured face. 'It's already won several New Zealand awards, and a couple of overseas ones. Nick Harding commissioned it.'

At Cat's blank look he expanded, 'An amazing man— he started off in advertising, made a fortune and won awards, then moved on to set up the best and biggest Internet provider in New Zealand. He's coining money, and according to the financial press he's in the middle of a deal that's going to boost him right into the stratosphere. And he's still in his early thirties!'

Thirty-two, to be exact. Cat swallowed and nodded. The building on the other side of the street gleamed prosperously, a vast contrast to the drab suite of rooms in a run-down industrial complex on the outskirts of Auckland that had originally housed Nick's business.

Somewhere in this palatial new building, perhaps behind one of those windows, he was waiting for her.

Her heart thudded sickeningly and moisture collected in her palms. Apart from a few newspaper photographs, she hadn't seen Nick for two years. Would he have changed? Would he think she'd changed?

'Are you a visitor to Auckland?' the man beside her asked.

'No,' Cat returned, too tense to be polite.

Rebuffed, he said, 'Oh. Well, have a nice day.' He moved away, losing himself and his dented pride in the growing crowd.

Carefully Cat wiped her palms on her handkerchief. A quick glance at her watch showed that she still had five minutes.

A month after she'd married Glen, Nick had walked out on his executive position in Glen's advertising agency, turning his back on everything Glen had done for him.

'Bloody ingratitude,' Glen had stormed. 'I took him in off the streets, gave him the best education in New Zealand and then sent him overseas to university, made him what he is, treated him like a bloody crown prince—and he betrays me.'

Impossible to imagine Nick—tall, harshly good-looking, wearing his expensive clothes with casual elegance—living on the streets! Yet everyone knew the story. Still raw with guilt at the memory of her response to Nick's unsparing kiss, Cat had asked, 'If he was a street kid, how on earth did you meet him?'

Glen had shrugged. 'Well, he wasn't living on the street; he shacked up with some girl in a hovel.' For a moment he'd looked uncomfortable. 'He baled me up outside the agency one day and asked for a job. I said, "Why should I give you a job?" And he said, "Because you're the best, and I plan to be better than you one day." He was only fourteen, but I could tell he meant it. I liked that, so I sent him off to my old school.'

Cat, who'd had first-hand experience of the casual cruelty of adolescents at an expensive boarding school, had asked, 'How did he deal with that?'

'With style and arrogance,' Glen had said indifferently. 'Had everyone eating out of his hand within a week. I knew he would; I recognised that steely self-confidence straight away, and it took me only ten minutes to see that he was brilliant. He worked like a demon, graduating with the highest grades, an A bursary and a whole new set of social skills. Blazed through university like a rocket! Now he's thrown the whole lot away to go on a wild-goose chase into the internet. It's going to collapse, and he'll go down with it.'

But he hadn't. Nick had ignored the gossip, ignored Glen's frustrated anger, and shown that he knew how to use determination and his ruthless intelligence to push his fledgling company to heights beyond anyone's guessing. Within a few years he'd ridden the eagle to become a multimillionaire.

Now, no longer a player only in the South Pacific, he was expanding into communications technology. He was set, so one business writer had pronounced tritely but apparently truthfully, to conquer the world.

Glen, who'd respected power, had eventually welcomed him back into the fold, only to be killed a few months later in a car accident.

That was when Cat had discovered that he'd appointed Nick to oversee the trust he'd set up for her. Still numb from the double deaths—for her mother had died only a month before Glen—she'd been relieved when Nick had treated her with remote courtesy. Except, her inconvenient memory reminded her, for a few searing moments after the funeral, when what had begun as a comforting touch had been transformed into desperate passion.

That desperate kiss had sent her fleeing overseas, and the only communication she'd had with him since then had been via her solicitor.

Soft mouth tightening, Cat obeyed the familiar buzz of the crossing signal. Now it was time to face Nick Harding again, woefully unprepared as always. Clad in a silk suit three years out of date, she swallowed to ease her dry throat, but there was nothing she could do about the butterflies in her stomach; they threatened to mutate into a herd of dinosaurs as she turned into the splendid foyer of his headquarters.

Tensely, Cat gave her name to the receptionist.

After a discreet glance at the wedding ring on Cat's hand, the woman said, 'Mr Harding's expecting you, Mrs Courtald. Take the lift to the fourth floor and his personal assistant will meet you.'

His personal assistant was altogether more intimidating; elegant in a severe midnight-blue suit, she waited by the lift door, her face revealing nothing but polite enquiry. 'Mr Harding won't be long,' she said as she ushered Cat into an impressive ante-room. 'Can I get you some coffee while you're waiting?'

Cat's stomach lurched. 'No, thank you.'

Coffee grew on the hills of Romit, a large island to the north of Australia—delicious, fragrant coffee that drew its superb flavour from red earth basking beneath a tropical sun. Cat never drank it now without being propelled back to a land torn apart by a bloody civil war that had left thousands dead.

But Juana lived, and it was for Juana she'd come here. Another bubble of foreboding expanded slowly in her stomach.

'Do sit down,' the personal assistant urged. 'Mr Harding won't keep you waiting for long.'

Smoothing out her frown, Cat sat in a chair and picked up a magazine, glancing at it without registering a word. Desperation had driven her to this place; she'd been turned down by bank after bank, the loans managers shaking their heads with professional solemnity and refusing her with equally professional courtesy—and insulting speed.

A blur of motion lifted the hairs on the back of her neck. She looked up, her skin prickling.

Like a panther, all noiseless, graceful intimidation, Nick strolled into the subdued luxury of the office and surveyed her with flat, unblinking eyes burnished the tawny colour of old gold—eyes that flicked across her face, then down to the finger on which, driven by some obscure need for protection, she'd pushed her wedding ring. Unworn for the past year, it weighed her hand down.

Driven by a need to establish some sort of physical parity, Cat stood up. For a horrifying second she thought the floor lurched beneath her feet. He reached her just as she clutched the back of the chair and dragged a deep breath into her lungs.

His hand closed around her upper arm, lean fingers gripping hard. 'Careful!' he barked.

She froze.

Shock splintered in his eyes, but the flare of emotion lasted less than a heartbeat; almost immediately a smile, as aggressive as it was humourless, curled his beautiful, chiselled mouth.

Oh, God, she thought hopelessly. Memories of him were seared on her brain, carved into her heart. She'd never forgotten his voice—deep, textured, a voice that could turn instantly to ice. It had featured in her dreams, tormenting her through endless nights.

'Hello, Cat,' he said with chilling courtesy.

Although a little harsher in feature, even more brazenly handsome, he hadn't changed much. Broad-shouldered, narrow-hipped and long-legged, radiating male power and authority, Nick Harding still dominated every room he

walked into, taking up all the space and all the air, so that
she breathed quickly and shallowly while her heartbeats
thudded in her ears.

And he still looked at her with utter and complete contempt in his lion-coloured eyes.

Cat fought back a flash of mindless panic. How many
times in two years had she dreamed of meeting Nick again,
imagined it in loving detail in those drowsy moments between sleep and wakefulness when her defences were
down?

Hundreds.

And now it was happening and she couldn't think,
couldn't do anything but respond with helpless intensity.

Nothing had changed.

'Hello, Nick,' she said thinly, acutely aware of the personal assistant's glance sliding cautiously from Nick's
tanned, gypsyish face to Cat's clammy one.

He said, 'Come on through,' and stepped back to let her
go ahead. 'No interruptions, Phil, please.'

Tension sizzled across the ends of Cat's nerves as she
preceded him into his office and looked around. The se-
verely organised room shouted his success—massive desk,
state-of-the-art computer, tall bookshelves and black leather
chairs around a low table. Floor-to-ceiling windows looked
out over Auckland's harbour.

'Lovely view,' Cat said inanely.

'I'm glad you like it,' he returned with sardonic courtesy.

Furious with herself for giving him an opening for sarcasm, Cat found her gaze drawn to a painting. Not the usual
bland business print; this was an original oil of a naked
woman, her back to the artist. All that could be seen of her
face was the curve of her cheek. It had been painted by a
genius who'd imbued the banal pose with dark mystery and
threat.

And it had to be pure coincidence that the fall of hair shimmering over the woman's ivory shoulder and down her back repeated the colour of Cat's—the burnished red-brown of a chestnut.

Once hers had been as long as that; now it was short and feathery.

Nick's eyes were hooded, impossible to read, but the black brows lifted in cool irony. 'Charming. As always. Clever to choose a silk so blue it turns your eyes to pure cornflower.'

In spite of the pathetic contents of her wardrobe it had taken her an hour to decide on the suit. Trying to control the violent mixture of emotions that pulsed through her, she retorted, 'And you're as subtle as always.' She stiffened her spine. 'How are you?'

His insolent golden gaze mocked her. 'All the better for seeing you.'

Long-repressed anger came to her rescue. She said bluntly, 'I don't believe that for a moment.'

It gave her a quick satisfaction to see Nick's brows snap together, but the counter-attack was swift and brutal. 'How did you enjoy the traditional widow's therapy?' At her startled look, his smile turned savage. 'Although most widows might feel that two years roaming the fleshpots of the world is a trifle excessive.'

'Roaming the *fleshpots*?' she parroted indignantly.

His survey seared the length of her body. 'You didn't buy that pretty thing in Auckland.'

'I—no.' Glen had bought it in Paris.

The words stuck in her throat, and before she could get them out Nick nodded. 'When did you get back to New Zealand?'

'In February.'

His eyes narrowed. 'What have you been doing since then?'

'Finishing my degree.'

'Really?' he drawled. 'Do I congratulate a fully-fledged accountant?'

'If I pass my finals.'

'Oh, you'll pass,' he said easily. 'Your intelligence has never been in doubt.' The insult buried in the words tested the fragile shell of her composure. 'Sit down, Cat.'

When she'd seated herself he walked around to the other side of the desk and sat there. Cat's stomach jumped, but he said mildly enough, 'Accountancy seems an odd profession for someone like you.' He waited before adding with smooth insolence, 'Although perhaps not.'

'I like figures,' she said crisply. 'You know where you are with them.'

'Much neater than all those messy emotions,' he agreed with a hard smile. 'And so convenient for keeping track of your finances.'

The implication that gold-diggers needed money skills angled Cat's chin upwards. Shrugging to hide her hurt, she wished she was eight inches taller—as tall as his PA. Height impressed people who thought small, fine-boned women were ultra-feminine, and therefore stupid and greedy. 'Exactly.'

'So, to what do I owe the honour of this visit?' he said indolently.

There was no easy way to say it, so she settled for blurting it out. 'I need some money.'

His golden eyes hardened. 'Of course you do,' he replied scathingly, leaning back in his chair and steepling his hands—just like all the finance managers who'd already rejected her, Cat thought with a flare of temper.

Eyes half closed, he said, 'As the trustee of Glen's estate

I made sure your annual allowance was transferred to your account four months ago. You're not entitled to any more for another eight months.'

'I need an advance.'

'How much, and why?' he asked, silkily insistent.

'Twenty thousand dollars.'

She didn't know what she'd expected—outrage, anger, disgust? But none of those emotions showed in the harsh, good-looking face, although Nick's iron control over his face and body blazed a clear warning.

Almost gently he asked, 'Why do you need twenty thousand dollars?'

Cat opened her bag and extracted a photograph. Her fingers shook as she pushed it across the wide desk. 'She needs an operation.'

He glanced down. Surprise, then something like black fury replaced the glitter in his eyes. He looked up and asked in a level, almost soundless voice, 'Is she your child?'

'No!' Cat sucked breath into starved lungs.

This time he examined the photograph for long seconds before asking, 'So who is she, and why do you need twenty thousand dollars?'

'Her name is Juana.'

He lifted a dispassionate gaze. 'Are you sponsoring her? Because no reputable aid agency demands twenty thousand dollars—'

'I'm not sponsoring her. I'm *responsible* for her, and you can see why I want the money.'

Once more he looked down at the photograph. Still in that calm, toneless voice he said, 'I can see she needs surgery, but what has that to do with your request for an advance on your allowance?'

'She has a cleft palate,' Cat told him crisply. 'At first the doctor thought that she'd be fine with just the one operation to fix it and the hare-lip, but once they got her to Australia they realised she'd need ongoing surgery. They booked her in for the next operation when she was two, but she's grown so much she's ready now. In fact, to be entirely successful it has to be done within the next couple of months. And as she's from Romit, and therefore not an Australian citizen, everything has to be paid for.'

Nick noted the way her lashes hid her eyes, admired the artistic tremor in her voice. To give himself time to rein in the hot anger that knotted his gut, he got to his feet and walked across to the bookshelves.

Deliberately choosing the position of power, he leaned a shoulder against a shelf and surveyed the woman in front of him. Normally he never bothered with the techniques of intimidation—he didn't need to. Only with this woman did he craft every inflection in his voice, the movement of every muscle in his body.

He had to give her credit for nerve. After two years without a word she'd walked into his office as coolly as though she had a dozen valid reasons to demand this money, and she wasn't giving an inch even now.

Of course, a woman with her assets had no reason to doubt herself.

Not that she was exactly beautiful. Cat Courtald—significant that she'd gone back to her maiden name!—had matured into an intriguing, fascinating, infinitely desirable woman, one with the power to sabotage both his will and his conscience. But then, he thought with hard self-mockery, recalling the times he'd touched her, she'd always had that power.

It had to be something to do with tilted blue eyes that smouldered with a secretive, lying allure, and skin like ivory silk, and a passionate, sultry mouth—and that was just her face! Her body almost tempted him to forget that this delicate, sensuous package hid a woman who'd sold herself to his mentor for security.

His *rich* mentor, he amended cynically. Four years later she'd tearlessly watched Glen's coffin lowered into the ground, her tight, composed face a telling contrast to the grief she'd shown at her mother's funeral.

She got to her feet to face him, her body stiff with anger. 'I need the money for her, Nick, not for myself.'

This from a woman who'd never shown any sign of liking children! Yet, in spite of everything, he wanted to believe her. Like all good actresses she projected complete and total sincerity.

Her attempt to use the little girl in the photograph made him sick and angry.

'Sit down, Cat,' he said evenly, 'and tell me how you got involved with this child.'

After a second's hesitation, she obeyed, disposing her elegant limbs neatly in the chair before lifting her arrogant little nose and square chin to say in the voice that made him think of long, impassioned nights and hot, maddening sex, 'I made myself responsible for her.'

Hunger ripped through him, ferociously mindless. Furious at his body's abject response to that degrading, treacherous need, he turned and walked behind the desk. Hiding, he thought sardonically. 'Why?'

'She was born on the first of November last year.'

Nick frowned. 'So?'

'So it was exactly a year to the day after my mother died.' The colour faded abruptly from her skin, sharpening her features. Yet she said steadily, 'I was in Romit. Her mother died having her. I—I made myself responsible for her.'

Clever, he thought objectively, to choose Romit as the scene of this drama. Unable to do anything to stop the carnage, unable to get help to the victims, people had watched in worldwide anguish as the images of a savage civil war had flicked with sickening vividness across their television screens. Even now, with the rebels beaten and a peace-keeping force in residence, the people of Romit were the poorest of the poor. Residual guilt should certainly prise his hands from the pursestrings. 'I see. Which agency is organising this operation?'

'None.'

His mouth thinned. 'Only a total idiot would fall for a story like that,' he said callously. 'What do you really want the money for, Cat?'

The light died out of her eyes, leaving them a flat, opaque blue as hard as her voice. 'I knew you'd accuse me of lying, so I've brought my passport and a letter from the nun who runs the clinic where Juana's being cared for. Sister Bernadette's explained where the money will go and why it's necessary now.'

Whatever he'd expected, it wasn't this.

He frowned as she opened her bag and held out a battered envelope and her blue New Zealand passport. Her long fingers flicked open the pages. 'Here are the dates I went into Romit,' she said coldly, 'and came out.'

How would those fingers feel on his skin? Would they cling and stroke? A volatile, potent cocktail of guilt and desire charged his body.

Repressing it, he focused on the stamped pages. God, he thought, fighting back a chill of fear. 'What the hell were you doing in Romit in the middle of a civil war?'

'I was working in a hospital—well, it was more a clinic, really.'

The customs stamps danced before his eyes as he recalled the hideous stories that had come out of the uprising. 'Why?'

She stared at him as though he'd gone mad. 'I told you—I was working.'

'You? In a Third World country, in a hospital?' He laughed derisively. 'Pull the other leg, Cat.'

With a sudden twist of her body that took him by surprise, she got to her feet.

Automatically he followed suit. Before he could speak she said in a tight voice, 'Read the letter, Nick.'

'I don't doubt for a moment that it purports to be from a nun in a clinic somewhere on that godforsaken island,' he said curtly. 'Easy enough to fake, Cat. You must have forgotten who you're dealing with. What were you doing on Romit?'

She shrugged. 'After my mother and Glen died a friend suggested I go and stay with her on the island—her father was attached to one of the UN agencies.' She hesitated a moment. 'The clinic was next door to their compound and running on nothing. When the fighting started at the other end of the island refugees poured in and they were desperately overworked at the clinic, so Penny and I helped. Then her father was pulled out; he insisted she go with him, but I stayed.'

'Why?' he asked harshly.

She stood with her head averted, hands held clenched and motionless by a fierce will. Outside a cloud hovered across the sun. In spite of everything, Nick had to stop himself from taking three strides and pulling her into his arms.

'I don't know,' she said at last in a muted voice. 'They were—are—so valiant. They had nothing at all, but they laughed and they were kind to each other and to me. The children liked me. And I had no one else.'

Oh, she did it well. Cynically he thought that she was

lucky; those fragile bones made every man long to protect her.

Furious at his weakness, he said, 'Couldn't you get out? The Cat Withers I knew would have run like hell in case something happened to her pretty little hide.'

'Courtald,' she flashed back at him. 'I'm Catherine Courtald! And you don't know anything about me—you never did. You looked at me and your prejudices sprang into life without reason or logic!'

'I had reason,' he said caustically. 'Or are you going to tell me that you were passionately in love with Glen when you married him—that you didn't even think that with his money you could take care of your sick mother and secure your own future?'

She flushed violently, and her gaze fell, her thick lashes hiding her eyes. 'I told you then—I was in love with him,' she said in a stifled voice.

'How could you be, when you looked at me and you wanted me—almost as much as I wanted you?'

'Have you never done anything stupid?' she demanded, squaring her shoulders.

'Yes. Six years ago I looked at my best friend's fiancée and lusted after her,' he said cruelly.

The colour fled from her skin. She made an abrupt gesture, then forced her hands back by her sides, her face into an exquisite mask.

Yet he still wanted to believe her. He strove to control the repressed lust and angry remorse—and a debilitating urge to shelter her.

Aloud he said, 'It's a good story, Cat, and you've done your research well, but I'm afraid I'm finding it very difficult to believe a word of it.' He flicked the photograph. 'Or a picture of it.'

Sheer stubbornness kept Cat upright. She couldn't go to

pieces now; she'd never forgive herself—or Nick—if his dislike and distrust stole Juana's future.

'Why don't you at least make an effort to find out whether I'm telling the truth?' she asked woodenly, picking up her bag. 'You can take the money out of next year's income.'

He lifted his brows. 'Twenty thousand dollars? What would you live on? Unless you're planning on finding another rich man to marry,' he said, adding with pointed courtesy, 'But as your trustee I have to remind you that if you do that you give up any further claim on Glen's estate.'

'I'm planning on finding a job,' she said between her teeth, and walked across the room.

Without looking at him, she closed the door behind her with precision, listening to the sound reverberate off every shiny surface.

Forcing herself not to flee cravenly, she nodded at the elegant, startled PA, who was hurriedly getting to her feet at her desk, took the lift down and strode out into the sunlight, greedily soaking up the heat. Chills rose through her, tightening her skin so that she felt as though she was suffering from a fever.

Nick Harding fever, she thought desperately. It hadn't gone away after all—instead it had lodged like a deadly virus inside her, waiting for one look, one touch, to set her afire again.

For heaven's sake, woman, get a grip, she commanded. You have to work out what you're going to do if he refuses to advance you that money.

Whatever happened, however she raised the money, Juana was going to have her chance.

CHAPTER TWO

A TENSE week later Cat was walking out of the university library when her companion nudged her and growled, '*Whooor!* Fantasy fodder at eleven o'clock.'

It was Nick, leaning indolently against a long, low car of the sort that had even the carefully sophisticated students looking sideways.

'What's my favourite colour?' her companion asked rhetorically. 'The colour of the last piece of clothing that man takes off in my bedroom!'

Cat unclenched her teeth to say with a lightness she hoped sounded real, 'Sinead, you've already got Jonathan—don't be greedy. Anyway, this one would break your heart.'

'Hearts mend, and from the look of him it'd be a wild affair, the sort you shock your great-grandchildren with.' She stopped as Nick straightened up and scrutinised Cat. 'Hey, you know him?'

The spring sun beat down on Nick's black head, glowed lovingly along the high, flaring cheekbones. He looked like a pirate—ruthless and forceful.

'I know him,' Cat said. 'Not well, but enough to be very wary.'

'If you don't want him, introduce me?' She laughed at the glint Cat couldn't banish from her eyes. 'It was worth a try. Go on, off you go—you can tell me all about him tonight.'

Alone, Cat walked over to the car, shoulders held stiffly, her face composed.

Nick's dark suit clung with the finesse of superb tailoring to his wide shoulders and narrow hips, but the formidable assurance and the slow burn of danger came from him alone.

Foolishly, Cat wished she'd worn her pretty blue suit again; jeans, even when topped by a cream shirt and a jersey the colour of her hair, couldn't live up to his clothes.

'Hello, Nick,' she said as she came up to him, her voice so constrained she sounded like a prim schoolgirl.

His mouth curved into a speculative smile. 'Cat.' He pushed the door open and held out a hand for her bag.

After a moment's hesitation she handed it over.

'This is far too heavy for you,' he said, frowning, as he dumped the bag in the back seat.

'Books always weigh a lot. Where are we going?'

'Somewhere that isn't quite so public as this.'

She nodded and slid past him into the car, folding her hands in her lap with a stern mental command to them to stay still. Resolutely she kept her eyes fixed straight ahead, although she registered nothing of the streetscape until they arrived at an elderly Art Deco apartment building beside one of Auckland's mid-city parks.

'This isn't your office,' she said sharply.

He switched off the engine. 'No.'

Just one word, but she sensed there was no moving him.

When she reached for her bag he said, 'It's all right where it is. I'll take you home later.'

At her straight look he smiled, a cool, intimidating smile that pulled every tiny hair on her body on end. He was up to something—but what?

'I'll bring it anyway,' she said evenly.

'Then I'll carry it.' He hauled the bag out in one smooth, powerful movement.

The modernised lift whisked them up quickly and silently, but once inside Nick's apartment Cat noted that the high ceilings and worldly charm had been left intact.

Nick ushered her into a huge sitting room that over-looked a sea of budding branches in the park. The usual municipal obsession with neat rows of flowers hadn't pre-vailed there; instead, showered by soft pink petals from a cherry tree, a graceful marble goose acted as a fountain, standing in a pond bordered by clumps of irises and freesias and small, starry, silver-blue flowers.

Grass stretched to a line of oaks; a few weeks previously they'd exploded into huge lime-yellow ice-creams and were now settling down with a dignified, dark green mantle. Their branches stirred with austere beauty in the lazy wind that was all this unusually warm season could produce.

Just keep your cool, Cat told herself, swallowing to re-lieve the stress that had built up beneath her breastbone.

'Can I get you something to drink?' Nick asked.

'No, thank you.' Not even though her mouth and throat felt as dry as the Gobi Desert.

'I'm thirsty, so excuse me,' he said abruptly, and dis-appeared through a door.

Tensely she looked around the room. If Nick had chosen the furniture he'd made a good job. It suited him, the pro-portions matching both the big room and his height and presence, but the black leather chairs and sofas, the exqui-site Persian rug and the stark abstracts on the wall, intim-idated her.

This, she thought distractedly, was how children must feel—helpless, ineffectual in a huge adult world.

Well, small she might be, but ineffectual she was not. Squaring her shoulders, she marched across to the book-shelves, oddly cheered when she noted some well-thumbed favourites of her own.

She was glancing through one when Nick returned with

a tray. Setting it down on the table, he said, 'I made some for you too. Sit down and pour, and for heaven's sake stop looking at me with the whites of your eyes showing. I'm not going to leap on you.'

With a distrustful glance, Cat put the book down and lowered herself onto a cold, smooth leather chair. At least the coffee gave her restless hands something to do. She poured his as he liked it, black and strong and fierce, and added a lot of milk to her own.

Nick had seated himself opposite, long legs stretched out. Accepting his cup, he asked, 'Why did you go back to your maiden name?'

Startled, she kept her gaze on the milky surface of her coffee. 'I wanted to.'

It was the wrong answer, but with Nick there were no right ones.

'You still wear his ring on occasion.' Smile hardening into contempt, his gold eyes flicked over the telltale lack of white skin on her bare finger. 'No doubt only when it's expedient to remind me that the man you married gave me a future.'

Shamed heat burned her cheeks; she'd used the ring as a talisman because it gave her the illusion of safety. 'Then you should understand how I feel about Juana. Glen gave you a future; I want to do it for her.'

'That's very clever, Cat,' he said softly. After a taut silence he went on, 'I checked with the clinic. What whim persuaded you to take responsibility for the child?'

Filled with a strange reluctance, she muttered, 'She only had an aunt—her mother's sister Rosita, just fourteen. Her father had been killed by the insurgents and I don't know what happened to the rest of her family. Rosita couldn't, or wouldn't, say.'

'That hasn't answered my question.' When she didn't go

on he probed uncompromisingly, 'What made the baby your responsibility?'

'Rosita had no money and no way of earning any. They were refugees. I couldn't just let the baby die when I knew she could be saved.'

He frowned. 'How did you find out about her?'

'I was there when she was born. I held her while the doctor tried to save her mother.' She gave him a swift glance from beneath her lashes, but his face was stern and unreadable. 'And she was special because she was born on the day my mother died. It seemed—significant, somehow. Symbolic.'

She waited for a sneer, for anger, but none came.

He was watching her through half-closed eyes, his mouth an unreadable line. 'Do you want to adopt her?'

She shook her head. 'Sister Bernadette convinced me she'll do better in her own culture with an aunt who loves her. Juana is all that Rosita has left—the only thing she has to live for.' Cat lifted her cup and drank some of the hot liquid, then set the cup down and looked him straight in the eye. 'I want to make sure she has all the surgery she needs—the doctors in Brisbane said there'll be at least a couple more operations, and she might need a dental plate too.'

'How long will all this take?'

'At least five years.'

'A long-term commitment,' he said coolly. 'And after that?'

'At the very least I'm going to make sure Rosita gets onto her feet somehow, so she can continue to care for Juana. Life for a girl with no family, no one to protect her, is difficult in Romit.'

'So you're planning the future of two girls?'

'Yes, I suppose so.'

Silence hummed between them, heavy with unspoken thoughts. Nick said quietly, 'In his will Glen made it impossible for me, as the trustee, to advance you any more than your yearly allowance.'

Cat bit back a protest; she'd been so shocked after Glen's death that she hadn't taken in much of what the solicitor had explained to her. Glen had always seen her as the naïve adolescent he'd swept off her feet, so his refusal to trust her didn't surprise her as much as it dismayed her.

Nick said deliberately, 'You could always ask me to help you.'

Why did suspicion darken her mind with ugly speed? 'I have asked you. You've just refused.'

'I can't ignore Glen's instructions. However, he trusted me to look after you.' He looked down at the letter and her passport. 'I could make you a personal loan. Or a gift.'

For a moment hope clutched her, but one glance at his hard, hunter's face killed it. She said with icy, desperate precision, 'For a price, no doubt. What do you want in return?'

'Perhaps I don't want anything,' he said, his eyes gleaming with a predatory light.

She gave a cynical little laugh. 'I doubt that very much. That's not how things work.'

Unblinking, he surveyed her. 'What are you prepared to give?'

More than anything she wanted to lick her dry lips, drink some more coffee to ease the passage of words through her arid throat. 'I only *give* to the people I love,' she said.

'By your own admission, you've broken that rule twice. Three times if we accept that you didn't love Glen when you married him.'

Colour burned her skin but she met his cold, golden gaze unwaveringly. 'But I did love him.' Because she'd been a starry-eyed innocent, dazzled and overwhelmed by Glen's sophistication.

'Setting aside your marriage to Glen, the other incidents were certainly errors of taste.' His voice was level, almost amused, but each word flicked her on the raw. 'After all, it's *not done* to make passionate love to—'

'We didn't make passionate love—we kissed; that's all,' she interrupted, hot-faced and shamed. 'And there were two of us—'

'Oh, there were indeed two,' he returned roughly. 'You and me, kissing as though we wanted to make love right there and then, the day before you married Glen, and the day we buried him.'

Coffee splashed over the edge of the cup onto her hand; Cat dragged in a shuddering breath.

'Have you scalded yourself?' Nick demanded, leaping to his feet to crouch by her chair. 'Let me see.'

He removed the coffee cup from her grip and set it down on the table. In spite of the sunny room ice froze Cat down to her bones.

'Just as well you drink it with a lot of milk,' he said, and lifted her stinging hand to his mouth as though he couldn't stop himself.

Cat's throat constricted. Dazed, she stared at him with dilating eyes, watching his lashes fall as his beautiful mouth touched the fragile skin of her wrist. Her fingers curled at the warmth of his mouth and sensation poured through her—hot, languid, remorseless as a river breaching its banks.

Shudders racked her body when she tried to pull away, but her strength had gone. She knew what he saw when he looked at her face—drowsy eyes and seeking, sensuous mouth—and she expected his slow, bitter smile. Hunger banished everything but a stark, stripped need; his angular features were stamped with it, the amber eyes smouldering, and his mouth—oh, God, his mouth...

She'd tried so hard to forget how it had felt on hers; for years she'd lied to herself, refused to accept that her desire for this man had never died. Unwanted and baseless, the treacherous physical attraction still burned inside her.

At eighteen she'd known too little of men to understand that Nick had been caught up in the same powerful attraction—until he'd kissed her and she'd gone up in flames, for the first time understanding the force of explosive sexual hunger.

Shocked and afraid, she'd turned her back on it, because she'd been naïvely certain it meant nothing compared to her respect and affection for Glen. During her marriage she'd banished Nick from her mind, only to crash and burn in the powerful force-field of that elemental hunger after Glen's death. The kiss after his funeral had begun as an attempt to comfort Nick—and ended when he'd pushed her aside and walked white-faced out of the house.

Nick hated himself for those endless moments in each other's arms. Cat understood; his regard for the man who'd given him his chance in life meant that there was no possibility of any future for them.

Not then, not ever.

Still with her hand against his mouth, Nick said harshly, 'Cat.'

He stood up, pulling her with him, and kissed her, and again it was like being spun into some alternative reality where the only thing that counted was Nick's mouth and his hard body against her, and the mingled scents of coffee and the musk of arousal.

And then she was free, clutching her shaking arms around her, and he was watching her with a guarded face, no expression on it at all.

'Damn you,' he said sardonically, 'you still kiss like a virgin.'

'And you,' she hurled back, 'still kiss as though you know exactly what you're doing, as though it's part of some plan.'

'It was never my plan to want you. At first I told myself that it was that patrician little face, those impeccable manners, that background. Not much money, but birth and breeding by the century.' His smile was cynical. 'An untouchable princess, irresistible to a boy from the streets.'

She said shakily, 'That's incredibly offensive.'

'But true.' He turned away, reached for the coffee cup and pushed it towards her. A muscle flicked in his jaw, and leashed tension prowled through him like a baulked tiger. 'Drink up.'

Her heart cramped. Ignoring the coffee, she started to leave. 'This is getting us nowhere; I'd better go.'

He shrugged. 'If you want that money, you'd better stay.'

Cat hesitated, hating this, hating him, but eventually she sat down again. She'd made herself responsible for Juana and she'd stick it out whatever it cost in pride.

Nick said with scathing honesty, 'Can you look me in the face and tell me you don't want me?' He waited, and when she remained stubbornly silent he finished, 'And that you don't hate being imprisoned by such a degrading desire? You resent it as much as I do.'

Cat's fingers tightened around the mug of coffee; any denial would be a lie. She lifted the cup to her mouth and drank the liquid, longing for the caffeine to kick in. She could do with some artificial support.

Nick let the silence stretch on until she said stiffly, 'Wanting is not enough.'

He laughed without humour. 'It's all we've got, Cat.'

Nothing had changed.

All they had in common was this driving sexual urge and money, she thought distastefully, trying to banish the image of Juana's face from her mind, because the sex would be wonderful, and the money would give the child a future.

She watched the coffee swirl as she turned the cup back and forth. Scraps of thoughts jostled and pushed in her brain, coloured by emotion's false hues, patternless and inchoate until one gained form, tantalising her into wondering if this was a chance to make Nick see her as she really was...

Seductive, alluring, the possibility filled her mind, banishing prosaic common sense.

Nick paced over to the window and stood staring out at the park, completely at home in the room he'd earned with determination and discipline and a huge expenditure of energy. From somewhere outside a horn tooted, followed almost immediately by the clear, liquid call of a thrush.

He said remotely, 'I'd give you fidelity, but I'd expect it too.'

Did he know Glen had been unfaithful, the first time within a year of their marriage when she'd insisted on going to university? Glen hadn't been a good loser.

Nick turned and looked at her, amber eyes missing nothing.

'No,' she said aloud, making up her mind in a flash of anger. She might have developed a taste for danger, but she was worth more than this! 'I won't have an affair with you, Nick, so that you can get me out of your system. I'm not some kind of disease you can inoculate yourself against. Yes, I want you, but I'm not going to sleep with you to scratch an itch that won't go away. I can do without you. I'm making a good life for myself; I'm settled and contented—'

'Contented!' He came across and took the mug from her, setting it down on the table. 'Contentment is for cows!' Eyes narrowed and hard and bright, he touched her face, long fingers stroking her cheek, easing down the line of her throat. 'You're so lovely,' he said, his voice dropping several notes, 'and when you smile you light up the world. Smile for me, Cat.'

His words melted her defences like flames on ice. Although she fought it, the beginnings of a fugitive smile curled her lips.

'And when you say my name,' he murmured, drawing her closer, 'it sounds like "I want you". I like to hear you say it, like the way you look at me when you think I can't see you...'

He bent his head until his mouth was a fraction away from hers and she could feel the words as he said them. 'The tiny flutter in your throat drives me crazy, and so does the colour that stains your skin, the way those exotic eyes go heavy and smoky and seductive when you look at me....'

By then she was desperate for him, her body so keenly attuned to his voice, to the faint fragrance that was his alone, to the shimmering sexual aura surrounding them, that she couldn't have refused the kiss.

Stark self-preservation clamped her eyes shut, and once she'd blocked out his face she could summon the energy to say hoarsely, 'I will not prostitute myself, not even to help Juana.'

'Why not? You prostituted yourself for your mother.'

Eyes flying open in shock, she whispered, 'I did not!' As his brows lifted she said lamely, 'It wasn't like that.'

'If she hadn't suffered from a heart complaint that meant she needed twenty-four-hour care, would you have married Glen?' Nick's voice was remote, his cloak of control pulled around him so that she could no longer guess at the emotions that lay beneath. He dropped his hand and stepped back, watching her with the merciless calculation of an enemy.

'If your father hadn't just died, leaving you penniless, would you have married Glen?' he probed unsparingly. 'You were alone and adrift, with a sick mother, no house, no job, and, thanks to some pretty antiquated ideas of child-rearing, no idea of how to find anything that would pay more than the most basic wage. When Glen came along like a slightly tarnished knight waving a chequebook, you saw deliverance and you couldn't marry him fast enough.'

She said indistinctly, 'My reasons for marrying him are none of your business.'

'Would you have left him at the altar if I'd offered marriage, Cat?' he asked cruelly. 'Or perhaps you'd have found the offer of money more attractive.'

She had no answer. When he'd asked her to cancel the wedding he'd offered her nothing. The prospect of failing her mother, of betraying Glen, had filled her with appalled apprehension.

And she had really believed that she loved Glen.

'No,' he said with a smile that chilled her soul, 'of course you wouldn't have. I didn't have half the money he had.'

In a quick, acid voice she returned, 'None of this matters now. My mother's dead, and Glen is too. Forget I asked for the money, all right? Forget I came to see you. Make things easier for both of us and pretend I'm still on Romit.'

Desperately she headed for the door.

But before she got there Nick caught her by the arm, swinging her around to face him, the gypsyish face taut with arrogant anger. 'What have you spent your income from the trust on? Why are you living in a hovel with five other students? Why are you working in a backstreet restaurant to put yourself through university?'

'You *have* been busy spying since I saw you last!' She'd expected him to check out her time in Romit, but the discovery that he'd run a survey on her since she'd got back to Auckland fuelled a feverish rage.

So angry that she could have slapped his face, she grabbed his shoulders and shook him. It was like trying to move a kauri, the largest tree in the southern hemisphere. 'Keep out of my life, Nick.'

'You invited me back into it.' But his voice had changed—become deeper, less furious.

The fingers around her arm eased their grip and slid up to her shoulder just as Cat realised that she'd got herself into an extremely perilous situation. Run! prudence yelled, but she couldn't let him go. Instead her hands moulded the sleek, firm muscles across his shoulders.

Eyes glinting, he said, 'You made the first move, Cat,' and kissed her, and this time she went under like a stone dropped into still, deep waters.

Always previously there had been anger and a driving desperation in his kiss; this time the anger was muted, soon replaced by a hunger that roused both urgency and an avid need—a potent, ferocious combination against which she had no defences.

Sensation tore through her; in a surrender as symbolic as it was unconscious, she opened her mouth to his, shuddering with pleasure when he accepted her yielding response and plundered the innermost reaches of her mouth, his arms tightening around her as he picked her up.

His mouth branded the length of her throat, summoning a raging tempest from every part of her singing, exultant body. Suddenly the progression from desire to passion, and thence to fulfilment seemed so simple, so natural and inevitable, tempting Cat unbearably with its honeyed promise of rapture.

His face against her throat was hot, his mouth demanding, yet she had never felt so safe, she thought dazedly, registering with a violent shock the touch of his hand on her breast, confident, overpoweringly erotic.

She shivered as passion needled exquisitely through her; expectant, breathless, she waited while he cupped the gentle curves.

And she knew she had to stop it now, while there was still time.

'Cat,' he muttered, the word slurred and heavy.

Summoning every ounce of will-power, she put her hands on either side of his face, lifting it until she could meet his eyes. 'No,' she said as distinctly as she could.

And watched helplessly as icy self-control drowned the golden turbulence of his eyes. He set her on her feet and stepped back, looking down at his hands as though they had betrayed him.

Grief proved greater temptation even than desire; shivering, she stopped herself swaying towards him.

'It won't work,' she said raggedly, stepping out of the danger zone. 'I'm going home.'

'I'll take you.' He ignored her headshake, picking up her bag.

Silently Cat went with him down to the car. She didn't give him her address, and he didn't ask; he drove straight to one of the few old houses in the inner city still divided into students' apartments. Cheap, dilapidated, it was close to the university and the restaurant she worked in at night.

'Did you know this place is due for demolition?' he asked as he braked outside it.

'Something else your spy discovered? Yes, I knew.' His dark frustration beat at her as she slid out of the car and pulled her bag out of the back. 'Goodbye, Nick,' she said in a calm voice that hid the painful thudding of her heart.

He didn't start the car until she looked out from her bedroom window.

Whenever she'd seen him she'd watched Nick secretly, imprinting on her too-susceptible heart the exact shade of his eyes, the way his lean cheek creased when he smiled, the sheer male grace with which he walked, the inborn aura of power that shimmered around him.

Yet somehow she'd managed to convince herself that her absorption meant nothing. She'd tried so hard to be a good wife that she'd lost herself, concealing the real Cat beneath the glossy surface of Glen's wife.

How foolishly naïve she'd been. Impressed, secretly proud that someone like Glen could fall in love with her, she'd let herself be persuaded into a marriage that had been fake from the moment she'd seen Nick. Would she have abandoned Glen if Nick had made some move towards her, had followed up on the potent attraction that spun itself between them? If he'd claimed her instead of standing back that day at the hotel?

One hand clenched at her side, she turned away from the window. She'd never know.

CHAPTER THREE

'IF THAT man at table six calls me girlie one more time,' Cat said viciously, 'I'll pick up what's left of his Thai lamb and pour it and the crisp noodle salad down the back of his neck.'

Sinead gave her a sympathetic smile. 'I think he's trying to impress his girlfriend.'

'From the way she's giggling and simpering,' Cat snorted, 'she already thinks he's the greatest wit of the millennium, so he can stop it right now.' Swiftly, competently, she began to assemble another salad.

'I'm glad he's yours,' Sinead said, tearing off her sheet and spiking it in front of Andreo, owner and chef in the small family restaurant, who was stir-frying.

After a quick glance he grunted acknowledgment, and said, 'Mind your temper, Cathy. If he touches you, yell all you like, but otherwise keep him happy. We want all the customers in those flash new restaurants down at the yacht basin to come back once the regatta's over and the billionaires have taken their super-yachts off to the West Indies, or wherever they migrate to at this time of year. If you make a habit of tipping good food over customers, it'll get around.'

'It's a severe temptation,' Cat said dourly. Working here had certainly opened her eyes to the many and varied types of humanity that existed in the only large city in New Zealand.

The soft tinkle of the doorbell sent her into the restaurant. She stopped suddenly, meeting the lion-coloured eyes of the tall man at the desk. A fierce, angry pleasure stained her cheeks, sent her heart soaring.

With an effort that probably showed in her face, she pinned a smile to her face. 'Table for one, sir?' she asked sweetly.

Unsmiling, Nick looked down at her. In black trousers and a black shirt—casual yet sophisticated—he was a creature of the night, dangerous, disturbing, his sexuality open and elemental. 'Yes.'

Cat picked up both menus and escorted him to a table set for two, whipping away the extra silver as he sat down. Concentrating on a point a little higher than his shoulder, she put the menus in front of him and recited the specials. It was difficult to ignore the excitement humming through her but she thought she managed, although she couldn't do anything about the colour burning along her cheekbones.

He didn't look at either menu. 'What's the best dish?'

'The fillet of beef with ratatouille and herb salad is particularly good, sir.' Dicing with danger, she thought as he looked up, his eyes gleaming gold fire. Excitement stroked along her skin, surged through every cell.

'Then I'll have that, and scallops for an entrée,' he drawled.

'Would you like a drink, sir?'

He shook his head. 'A beer will do.' And named one of the boutique beers they stocked.

'Yes, sir,' she said.

When she brought the beer he thanked her and lifted his gaze to her face. 'Don't call me sir,' he commanded, steel running through the words.

An odd sensation slid down her spine. 'It's traditional,' she countered.

'That's not why you're doing it.'

From behind her came a cry of, 'Girlie! Girlie! Where's that waitress?'

'Excuse me,' she said, almost giddy with relief, and scrambled back to the man at table six and his giggling girlfriend.

'You've made a mistake with this bill,' he said loudly. 'I've checked it on my calculator and you've charged me an extra seven dollars.'

It took some minutes for her to go through the orders with him, show him that they were down on the bill, and get him to run it past his calculator again, this time with the result that appeared on the bill.

Of course he didn't say he was sorry.

'And I'll bet he didn't tip, either,' Sinead muttered, keeping an alert, fascinated eye on Nick.

'I didn't expect him to. Why should he? Tipping's not a New Zealand custom,' Cat said, keeping *her* eyes on the till as she ran another bill through it. 'Not unless we do something outstandingly wonderful for the customer.'

'You didn't kill this one, which I think was outstandingly wonderful of you! Anyway, your tall, dark and handsome didn't like it when that guy made a fuss,' the other woman said with relish. 'Talk about filthy looks!'

'You're imagining things. He's not mine.'

'That may be so,' Sinead said cheerfully, 'but from the way he watches you I'd say he thinks of you as very much his.'

'Don't be silly,' Cat said ineptly.

'Oh, Cat, sometimes I think you're the sweetest little old maid in disguise!' Laughing, Sinead patted her on the head. 'Live a bit, why don't you? Look at him! He's very cool and thoroughly all right in a plutocratic sort of way—just the sort of guy to give you a really good time. Who is he? I feel I should know him.'

'Nick Harding,' Cat said without emphasis.

'So is he your boyfriend?' Clearly the name meant nothing to her.

'No.'

'Hmm.' Sinead was studying art. She lowered her voice and said with relish, 'Splendid bones. Good clothes sense too—black suits him superbly. And I do admire that louche, untamed air—all smouldering and intense and yet somehow ferociously disciplined. I'll bet he's so utterly dynamic in bed.'

'Have you ever thought of changing your major?' Cat enquired, alarmed by a knife-slash of jealousy. 'To creative writing, perhaps? And what about Jonathan, who is probably even now revving up his motorbike so he can take you to a nightclub?'

Sinead chuckled. 'All right, you saw him first—but, hey, a girl can dream, can't she?'

Ten minutes later she hissed, 'I've just realised who Nick Harding is.' She paused and when Cat raised her brows, she probed, 'I presume he *is* the Internet zillionaire?'

'Yes.'

Sinead picked up a pepper grinder. 'Makes you rethink all the definitions of computer nerd, doesn't it? He looks like some swashbuckler from the days when buckles were swashed as a regular thing. Hunk doesn't apply—too everyday. Unfortunately I don't think there's a word that means good-looking as sin, with an edge of ruthlessness and danger.' She winked at Cat. 'I sense hidden depths and dark secrets and a certain wild recklessness that sets my hormones buzzing. Why, I wonder, isn't he down at the yacht basin with all the other billionaires and high society people? Could it have anything to do with your mysterious, slanted eyes?'

Grinning triumphantly, she carried the grinder off.

Cat was on edge for the rest of the evening, even after Nick had drunk his beer, eaten his dinner, and left with no more than a nod. He didn't try to tip her, which was a relief; she would, she thought vengefully, have flung it back in his face, and then Andreo would have had a fit.

It was late when she finally stepped out onto the footpath outside the restaurant, waving Sinead and her Jonathan off on his motorbike.

'No, you don't have to see me home,' she told them when they hesitated. 'Go and dance all night!'

'You're sure?' Sinead peered at her.

'Dead sure. When has there ever been a mugging here? Off you go.'

Sinead seemed as though she was going to insist, but then she looked past Cat and gave a quick nod. 'OK, see you tomorrow!'

They took off and she turned and walked briskly away. The sky hung low, threatening rain on a warm wind from the tropics. Because Auckland was spread across on an isthmus between two harbours, one on the west coast, one on the east, every wind and breeze came salted with the sea.

Other scents floated across from the Domain park—newly mown grass, some exotic perfume that hinted of the tropical plants sheltered in the elegant glass Wintergardens, and the sweet, potent fragrance of datura flowers behind a nearby hedge.

Although it was after midnight, traffic hummed along the motorway; Cat wished she could drive north as far as she could, and settle in some small town so far away from Nick that he'd never find her.

The sound of her name jerked her head up. A swift flare of excitement set her blood afire as she saw Nick walking around his long, sleek monster of a car. Had she summoned him just by *thinking* about him?

No wonder Sinead had gone off so happily!

'I'll drive you home,' he said. 'I hope you're not in the habit of walking by yourself at this hour of the night.'

'Sinead and I usually go home together.' Made uneasy by his closeness, Cat shrugged further into her jacket. 'We live in the same house.'

'Get in.' When she hesitated, he said curtly, 'Unless you want me to follow you all the way home?'

Fuming, she obeyed, sitting in eloquent silence while he set the car in motion. If he touched her, she thought nastily, she'd hit him where it hurt most. She wasn't going to endure again the consuming lash of his sexuality and her own feral response. It was humiliating.

He made no attempt to touch her. They were almost at their destination when he said, 'Why, when you get a very adequate allowance from your trust fund, do you work every night at a second-rate restaurant?'

She bristled. 'Andreo is a superb cook—'

'That's not the issue,' he cut in incisively. 'Why are you so cagey? I assume the answer's got everything to do with the ecstatic answer I got from the clinic in Ilid. According to Sister Bernadette you are a major benefactor—in fact, the only benefactor the clinic has. Thanks to your generosity, she told me, they now own some piece of equipment I can't even spell, let alone pronounce.'

'It's a—' She bit back the words.

He drew the car to a halt outside the house. 'Yes, I thought you'd know all about it. How much did it cost?'

Cat stared at the dark window that indicated her shabby room. If she'd known Juana was going to need this second operation she'd have kept twenty thousand dollars back, but she couldn't regret that the clinic now had a functioning surgery ward and theatre.

Eventually she said, 'It's none of your business. All you

have to do is see that the income from the trust goes to the right place once a year.'

'If you think that's all a trustee does,' he said cuttingly, 'you should, perhaps, re-read the relevant pages in your textbooks. Glen certainly didn't intend you to send it all to a hospital in Romit. I don't need to tell you he'd be horrified to see his wife waiting in a restaurant, however good the chef. He wanted you to be taken care of.'

She said distantly, 'I can look after myself.'

Nick switched off the engine and turned to look at her, both hands still on the wheel. 'Not very well. You've got dark circles under your eyes.'

She remained stubbornly silent.

'All right,' he said, dismissing the subject, 'forget it. If it makes you happy, spend every cent you get on the clinic. I have a favour to ask of you.'

'A *favour*?'

Glen had used to grumble about Nick's damned, stiff-necked pride. Nick followed his own road with a self-contained authority and confident determination that got him where he wanted without asking for help. A sideways glance revealed his profile—granite-hard and uncompromising.

A flash of white indicated his narrow smile. 'You heard,' he said crisply. 'It won't be easy, and it will involve moving in with me. You've heard of the Dempster Cup, I assume?'

'I do read the newspapers,' she retorted, her heart lurching in her chest. Steadying her voice, she added, 'Next to the America's Cup it's the most prestigious yacht race in the world, and this year it's in Auckland. And so, of course, are all the rich people who follow rich yacht races in their super-yachts. What on earth does a sailing competition have to do with a favour from me?' In a tone edged with sarcasm, she added, 'Especially one that involves moving in with you.'

'Have you also heard of Stan Barrington?'

'The Australian media man? Glen used to talk about him, but I don't think I ever met him.'

Nick said coolly, 'He has a daughter who is looking for a husband. Both she and Stan think I would make an excellent one. I don't. However, I do need to keep on good terms with the old buccaneer.'

'A matter of business,' Cat said softly, wondering why she felt so depressed. This must be the deal the man at the street crossing had referred to—the one that was going to boost Nick into the stratosphere.

'Exactly.'

Although his hands still rested lightly on the steering wheel, his fingers were tapping it. Nick, who never asked favours, also never fidgeted.

As though he realised what he was doing, his fingers stopped. He said calmly, 'Francesca Barrington is a very determined woman, and I suspect she's not above manipulating circumstances to suit her. She probably won't be able to persuade her father to drop the discussions we're having, but I'm not going to give him a chance. Too many jobs depend on a satisfactory outcome, and, while I don't mind being beaten in a fair fight, I'm not going down to a foul like that. And I refuse to string her along and then dump her when it's all signed up.'

'Oh, no,' Cat said, horrified, 'no, you couldn't do that.'

'I'm glad we agree about something,' he said urbanely. 'What I need is a fiancée and I think you'd make an excellent one.'

'No!'

'Perhaps you're right,' he said with a thoughtful note in

the deep voice that set her teeth on edge. 'An engagement is far too formal. A lover would be better.'

She blurted, 'Why me? It would be——' Hot with embarrassment, she stopped.

'Dangerous,' he supplied laconically. 'You think we might give in to temptation and fall into bed together?'

Cat fought the urge to lick her lips.

'Would that be such a disaster?' The lights from a slow-moving car caught his face, travelled across the angular, slightly foreign features, the beautiful, sardonic mouth, and the heavy-lidded eyes.

Cat's stomach flipped and her spine melted; a violent tug at her senses sent a pulse of shuddery anticipation through her. 'Yes, it would be a complete and total disaster!' she said explosively.

The car hummed past, and in the darkness she heard him say, 'I prefer to indulge my power complex in more subtle ways than force.'

'You wouldn't... I'm not afraid of that!' The answer came without hesitation.

'Well, that's a comfort,' he said drily.

She couldn't tell him that she didn't trust herself to keep her distance. Nick knew how to take advantage of weaknesses. 'Why not pay an actress? Or ask a friend...?'

'I need someone I can trust.'

In spite of herself Cat felt a thrill of pleasure at this.

He drawled, 'You seem to have your little protégée's welfare very much to heart, and if you act convincingly I'll pay for her operation.'

Cat's breath hissed through her lips.

'If you don't,' he said uncompromisingly, 'she'll have to wait until the next instalment of your money from Glen's estate comes through.'

'By then it will be too late,' she said stonily.

'So I understand.' He let that hang in the air for a few seconds before saying thoughtfully, 'Francesca's not a fool. It's impossible to fake sexual attraction. With you installed in my house as my lover she won't have any doubt. And we know each other well enough to make a relationship hang together.'

Opening her mouth to speak, Cat found she had nothing to say.

'I'll support you while you're living with me,' he said in an even voice, 'and I'll help you get a decent job.'

'You will not!'

Cynically he said, 'That's how it's done, Cat—someone talks to someone else. It's not nepotism, and you won't be kept on if you can't do the work.'

'I can do any job I'd apply for,' she said steadily.

'I'm sure you can,' he said, a note of irritation roughening his voice. 'What's it to be—yes or no?'

She blustered, 'I can't make a decision just like that!'

'You'll have to,' he said ruthlessly. 'I've got arrangements to make. The Barringtons plan to be here in a week, and I want you in my life immediately so that you know your way around it.'

Temptation tormented her. Keeping her eyes on the dark window of her flat, she said, 'Don't try to steamroller me, Nick. I need to think about it.'

'Very well, you can have tonight,' he said, and got out, walking around the front of the car to open her door.

Cat had expected him to insist on an answer then; if he had, she might have been able to say no. But Nick didn't insist.

'You're not likely to get the money from the bank,' he said coolly, closing the door after she'd got out, 'not even with the trust fund to back a loan. Treasury has just announced that inflation is rearing its ugly head again, so bank managers are clamping down.' He stopped as though waiting for an answer, then Cat saw the thin white flash of his smile. 'But of course you know that—you've already tried to raise the money.' His voice altered. 'Promise me something.'

Groping in her bag for her keys, she said huskily, 'What?'

'That you won't go to a moneylender.'

She found the key and put it in the lock. 'I won't,' she said, turning the key and pushing the door open. She'd already tried moneylenders; they'd been as uncooperative as the banks, and not nearly so polite.

The hall had once been magnificently Edwardian, but many years of students and low rents had stripped it of any past glory. With peeling, stained wallpaper, and the floor covered by a strip of lino from the seventies, it not only looked sleazy, it smelt it as well.

'Goodnight,' she said.

'I'll pick you up for lunch tomorrow.'

For some reason she didn't want that. 'No.'

'All right—I'll meet you at Oberon's restaurant in Parnell at one o'clock. They do extremely good seafood. Open the window of your bedroom when you get there so I can see you've made it.'

Exasperated, she retorted, 'This is my home, not a den of iniquity! Goodnight,' and walked swiftly away, up the stairs and into her room, stepping over an envelope that someone had pushed under her door.

She heaved the warped window up, dragging in a breath of petrol-scented air. Below, in the gravel yard that had once been a garden and still had an untidy fringe of vegetation, a tall, dark figure looked upwards and lifted a hand. She banged the window shut and watched in the darkness as Nick got into his car.

The prospect of staying at his house—pretending to be his lover—was terrifyingly alluring. Perhaps her months in Romit really had given her a taste for danger?

Shivering, she washed and shrugged into one of the roomy, comfortable T-shirts she liked to sleep in.

No, the danger in Romit had been very real, but it had been purely physical, whereas living with Nick would put her heart in the worst sort of jeopardy. The sensible thing would be to run as far from him as she could.

Why wasn't she over it by now? Lust died when it wasn't fed, and she'd tried so hard to starve this sexual chemistry into nothingness.

With an almost total lack of success. Whenever she saw Nick her body still sang with hidden rapture, a longing so deeply rooted in her that it was like a primal hunger. In her dreams she'd wondered if it was love; awake, she knew it wasn't.

Love entailed liking and respect, and although she'd learned to see past Nick's concealed antagonism and effortless authority, beyond his dangerous, persuasive charm to his basic integrity and intelligence and determination, she knew he didn't respect her at all.

As for liking her—forget it!

Was it cosmic irony, she thought, yanking the bedcover around her, or just bad karma that she should be so obsessed by Nick? Perhaps she was being punished for marrying Glen for all the wrong reasons.

She'd begun seriously wooing sleep when she remembered the envelope still lying on the floor inside the door. Groaning, she got up and pattered across the room, scooped up the envelope and scurried back to bed, switching on the bedside lamp. After the usual reluctant flickering, it steadied enough for her to read the brief note.

The house, the solicitor for the landlord informed her in

a businesslike way, had been sold for demolition, and therefore she was required to leave at the end of the following week.

Cat stared at the page; it was computer-generated, so the other residents would have identical ones. All university students, they'd soon be heading home to various parts of New Zealand, but she had nowhere to go.

Worse than that, her job at the restaurant would finish shortly, when Andreo's daughter came back from university at Dunedin.

For a moment sheer panic hollowed Cat's stomach, but only for a moment.

'Stop dithering and work out what to do!' she muttered, all hope of sleeping gone.

The letter drastically narrowed her options. A new flat meant money up front to pay the bond. By stringent economising she'd saved enough to tide her over the holiday season, when no firms were hiring, and by living economically and helping Andreo out when things got busy she'd expected to survive until her degree was certain and she could put the letters after her name on her CV.

Why on earth couldn't the wretched landlord have waited another six weeks before demolishing the house?

Casual jobs were practically impossible to get during the summer, when Aucklanders fled the humid city for cooler beaches and the Gulf. Still, she might be able to pick something up at the yacht basin. There might be other opportunities there as well, where her accountancy skills would be useful. She'd check out the newspaper in the morning.

Because the only other alternative was to accept Nick's outrageous offer...

'I'll cope,' she said stoutly, but she shivered as she crawled back under the covers, and once there lay for hours staring into the dark while the old house creaked and settled and her thoughts tumbled and fought for precedence.

In the end she decided to turn the problem over to her unconscious, and fell into a restless, dream-tossed sleep.

Her unconscious failed her. The next morning, still feeling like an animal herded inexorably towards a trap, she ate a morose breakfast before wandering outside, coffee mug in hand.

The temperature had risen overnight, turning the salty winds into a caress. In her few hours of sleep she'd dreamed of Nick—sexual, yearning dreams that still fired her skin with colour. Restlessness, made worse by a feeling of impending doom, drummed through her, compelling her to action.

She drained the coffee and set the mug down on the edge of the veranda. She should walk over the grassy slopes of the Domain—better still, bike to Mount Eden and exhaust herself by climbing that sharp, steep little volcanic cone. No, she should buy a newspaper and track down some employment.

She gazed around the forlorn remnants of a garden that had once been someone's delight, perhaps their comfort in moments of pain and indecision. It seemed wicked that in a few weeks the last struggling survivors would be bulldozed into nothingness. Her eyes fixed onto a clump of daylilies, the valiant orange flowers glowing through a choking mantle of weeds.

Cat got a knife from the communal kitchen, salving her conscience by telling herself she'd clean it carefully so no one would know.

Freeing the lilies was hard work, and as the sun climbed she began to sweat, but the difference her slashing and hacking made kept her at it.

Think logically, she told herself, yanking out another

strand of buttercup. Nick wants a favour, and he's prepared to pay for it. He's probably pretty confident that he can seduce you as an extra bonus.

As he had every reason to be. She'd been a total failure at rejecting him.

Resisting the sharp clutch of sensation in her stomach, she attacked a flourishing dock. The thought of being Nick's lover wove its own dark magic—a powerful, spellbinder's enchantment, perilous, exciting, infinitely tempting. She piled lush green leaves in a tidy heap with the other weeds and sat back, wiping her forearm across her forehead.

'I can handle myself,' she muttered.

But could she? And, more to the point, would she want to? Nick had never liked her, but he wanted her, a desire she returned with a helpless, hopeless hunger. Living in the same house would expose her mercilessly to that potent, overwhelming attraction. Why not just give in to it?

'The trouble is,' she told a harmless passing bee, 'that I've spent years resisting him in my mind.'

She stood up and surveyed the daylilies. In Auckland's warm weather the weeds would soon creep back, but for the moment the plants held up their gallant flowers to the sun for benediction.

A movement beyond the tattered hedge brought a smile to her face as she met the eyes of the elderly woman who walked past every morning to buy a newspaper.

The older woman nodded at the clump of daylilies. 'That looks much better—you've liberated the flowers. I love daylilies, don't you?'

'Yes, although I don't know why I've bothered,' Cat said wryly. 'The house is going to be demolished soon and they'll just bulldoze these out of the way.'

'Summer's here, so your sap's rising.' She gave a comfortable chuckle. 'Be careful, or you'll find yourself doing crazy things. Although, come to think of it, I don't regret any of the crazy things I've done. What I do regret are the crazy things I didn't do.'

Cat said, 'Why didn't you do them?'

'Because I was a coward.'

'But you can get so hurt.'

'Better than drying up because you lack courage.' She gave Cat a warm smile. 'Nobody with a vivid, wilful face like yours is going to give in to mediocrity. Grab life by the hands, girl—you can only guard your heart so far without draining all the juice from it. And don't worry about those daylilies. As soon as you all move out I'll nip in and dig them up and take them home. They'll be fine. Good luck, my dear. I'll miss your lovely smile and your pretty red hair.' She nodded and moved off towards the bus stop.

Slowly Cat heaped the pile of weeds into the bin and went inside. When she'd washed the knife and put it away, and was ready to meet Nick for lunch, she went to the window. Bold and bright, their heads held high, the daylilies stood proudly.

She hadn't made a conscious decision, but she knew that she was going to accept Nick's offer. If it all went wrong, she thought with grim honesty, she couldn't be any worse off than she was now—eating her heart out for a man who wanted her as much as he distrusted her.

A sudden jerky movement of her hands drew her gaze to the mirror beside the window; she stared at the woman who gazed back at her, eyes half closed, mouth curled in an intimate smile, a faint flush heating her skin.

Perhaps it wouldn't go wrong. Perhaps he'd learn that she was a reasonable human being, not a hard-hearted, greedy opportunist.

'And pigs might fly,' she said bleakly.

CHAPTER FOUR

NICK wasn't alone when Cat saw him outside the smart restaurant he'd chosen for lunch.

His companion—black hair in a sleek bob, superbly tailored black suit showing off a pair of long legs made even more shapely by black stockings and high-heeled black shoes—was laughing up at him, one slim hand resting intimately on his sleeve.

The colour drained from Cat's skin. It was stupid, she scolded, to be so affected! Nick usually had some lovely woman on his arm.

Nevertheless, she felt shorter than usual, and dowdy in her blue suit, and her quick sideways duck behind a potted tree two shops away was purely instinctive. Once safely hidden, she stared into a window display.

Light danced in her eyes, reflected from the mirrors that backed a sophisticated sweep of jewellery arranged with skill and restraint to make maximum impact. Keeping her eyes fixed fiercely onto the dazzle of gold and diamonds, she waited, refusing to go up to Nick while he spoke to another woman.

The chains and rings blurred, swam together. She swallowed, fighting down an outrage as humiliating as it was unwanted.

'Which one do you like?'

His voice—smooth, taunting—froze her. Skin tingling, her breath blocked in her throat, she stared at his reflection.

He wasn't touching her, but he was standing behind her so that he cut her off from the passers-by. His unsmiling face exuded a primal male power that contrasted blatantly with his classical dark suit and the polished gleam and shimmer inside the shop.

Nick's sophisticated surface hid a warrior; he wielded a warrior's raw strength and authority. In an arrow-flash of insight she understood that his uncivilised core drew her reckless, consuming response. She wanted him with a hunger beyond control, beyond understanding, because in some mysterious and elemental way they were linked.

'I don't like any of them,' she returned crisply.

'So why are staring at them with such interest?'

'I didn't want to interrupt your conversation.' Damn, did that sound as acid and bitter as it felt?

She glared at a particularly showy ring, as though by doing so she could weaken the pounding of her pulse.

With apparent idleness Nick asked, 'What's wrong with the jewellery?'

'It's too heavy, too obvious.'

'On your slim wrists and fingers, around your elegant throat, yes. That diamond ring in the centre would look spectacular on your finger. Would you like it?'

She looked up, met eyes as calculating as a computer.

Sweat began to prickle down her spine. If he openly offered her a position as his mistress she'd hit him right in the middle of his flat stomach—and then she'd fall to pieces. Her answer came swiftly, without conscious thought. 'No.'

'You could always sell it. That's the usual procedure, isn't it?' he said softly, amber-gold eyes measuring her reaction.

'I wouldn't know.' But she looked down, avoiding his gaze.

He probed, 'Where's the engagement ring Glen gave you?'

'Gone.' The word tasted acrid in her mouth. It had bought drugs and equipment that had saved lives in that small hospital in Ilid.

Nick had known she'd sold the ring; she read the knowledge in his eyes, in the cynical twist of his mouth. The skin across her shoulders tightened in elemental warning. Acutely, suffocatingly aware of his size, his height, she sensed a primitive menace more powerful for being so mercilessly leashed, yet every cell of her body throbbed with life. If she turned she'd be pressed up against him, hip to hip, thigh to thigh—

Glaring at the winking jewellery, she sternly resisted the memory.

'I hope you invested the proceeds wisely,' Nick said with smooth insolence.

'Why do you hate me?' The rash words tumbled out before she could close her lips on them.

He paused. Resisting the compulsion to look at him, Cat wondered despairingly when she was going to learn to keep her mouth shut.

'I don't hate you. In a way I quite admire you,' he drawled. 'You made the most of your considerable assets, used them wisely.'

'You resented me from the start.' She remembered how he'd looked at her with cold, unbending dislike when Glen had introduced them. 'Why?'

'Resentment? Yes, perhaps I did feel that.' The blandly speculative tone couldn't hide the flick of scorn. 'You were shy and demure, not at all my style. Yet I took one look at you and wanted you.'

Her hands jerked in a betraying movement.

'You knew,' he said, giving no quarter. 'What *would* you have done, Cat, if I'd offered to take you away, marry you?'

Her tongue stole out to wet her dry lips. Dithering, she waited too long to answer before blurting, 'I'd have said no. I'd made a promise to Glen.'

In a bored voice Nick said, 'And of course Glen was besotted with you, whereas I recognised what you were— to use an old-fashioned term, a gold-digger.' His smile was edged with cynicism. 'In the nicest possible manner, of course, and perhaps for the noblest of all reasons—your mother's welfare—but you were out for what you could get. Even if loyalty to Glen hadn't been an issue, I knew by then that I was going out on my own. I could have lost every cent I had. You were far more sensible to take him.'

His cool, judicial words hurt, as they were meant to. Furious, stabbed by a profound sense of betrayal, Cat beamed sunnily at his reflection, and said, not hiding the cool flick of scorn in her tone, 'It must be maddening that you still want me.'

He recovered swiftly from his surprise, the hot glitter in his eyes dying to an opaque sheen. 'Yes,' he said with a tight, angry smile. 'And you want me. It's an interesting situation.'

Cat's heart jumped, but her wildfire elation faded swiftly, leaving the taste of ashes in her mouth. A memory stood between them like a flaming sword, barring the way to any sort of closure, locking them into antagonism. Nick would never forget that he'd betrayed Glen with the kisses that had burned on Cat's mouth ever since.

'I find it exasperating rather than interesting,' she said, the dismissive words hiding, she hoped, her increasing need to get out of there.

Inside the shop a woman looked up from behind the counter. Her smooth hair—just a shade too pale to be natural—pulled back from a delicately made-up face, she'd been covertly watching them as she tidied a drawer of rings.

No, she'd been watching Nick. Women watched him all the time. His expensive, superbly cut business suit couldn't hide the promise of danger, the untamed energy that both excited and challenged.

A needle of jealousy stabbed Cat in the heart. He's mine, she thought suddenly.

Why not take what he offered? What did she have to lose? A consuming, risky affair would either burn out that elemental link between them—or prove that they were soulmates...

And what would she do then?

At least she'd know.

'That's an odd expression,' he observed.

She shrugged. 'Is it?' she parried casually. It took all her courage to add, 'I've made up my mind, by the way. I'll agree to your bargain.'

'What made you decide?' he asked coolly.

He didn't look surprised, or relieved or even satisfied. His expression remained controlled and unreadable, yet her body went on high alert; she shrugged and said even more casually, 'There's nothing else I can do.'

His lashes drooped, hiding his eyes, and the angular framework of his face seemed to clench for a fragment of time. Then he said, 'You'll pretend to be my lover in return for twenty thousand dollars?'

'Yes,' she said simply. And pretend was all she'd do.

Although temptation still danced in front of her, making promises as gaudy and tantalising—and far more alluring— than the jewellery, she knew that if she succumbed and had an affair with Nick, she'd be broken. She couldn't match his steely strength and she was too afraid of the havoc he'd create in her life to risk it.

She caught a glimpse of a clock at the back of the shop

and ostentatiously looked at her watch. 'Shouldn't we be going?'

He didn't move. Cowardice urged her to bolt down the footpath, around the corner and out of sight, to abandon any hope of helping Juana until the next annuity instalment. Pride held her still and erect.

A small child ran towards them, sturdy legs pumping as he laughed over his shoulder at the woman who chased him, calling out his name in fear. As he came level he tripped, face splitting into a roar.

Nick moved so fast that Cat cried out in shock; his deft hands scooped up the child before he hit the ground, lifting him and holding him safely against a broad shoulder. Gently Nick said, 'You're all right. Don't cry now.'

Wide eyes fixed on Nick's dark face, the little boy gulped, but swallowed back his tears.

'What's your name?' Nick asked as the child's mother— no, grandmother—arrived.

'Petey,' the child whimpered, mesmerised by the soothing note in the deep voice.

'Say thank you to the nice man,' his grandmother said, smiling gratefully at Nick.

A vice squeezed Cat's heart. She'd never seen Nick with a child before, and it suddenly seemed outrageous that in her life with Glen there had been no children. His friends didn't have them and he hadn't wanted them—in four years of marriage she couldn't remember any child in the huge, ultra-luxurious penthouse they'd shared.

Wide-eyed as Petey, she saw Nick hand him over to his grandmother. He said a few words that made the older woman laugh, and watched them walk down the street, returning the little boy's shy farewell with a wave of his long fingers and a smile like nothing she'd ever seen before from him. It hit her with the unyielding force of a sandbag to her midriff; she literally couldn't breathe.

'What is it?' he asked abruptly.

'Nothing.' Stepping away, she dragged in a ragged breath. 'Just admiring the speed of your reactions.'

'When you grow up waiting for the next blow, you tend to react very fast.'

Horrified, Cat looked up at him. 'I'm sorry,' she said stupidly. 'I didn't know.'

Dark features shuttered against her, he returned, 'I was lucky. I had friendly neighbours who welcomed me in when things got too much. Come on, let's go and eat.'

Washed by an enormous, useless tide of compassion, and a fierce anger at whoever had brutalised him, she went with him into the restaurant.

Inside they were shown to a discreet table behind some vigorous tropical growth, and when they'd both ordered Nick chose the wine.

'Champagne?' Cat queried into the taut silence when the waiter moved away.

'Why not? It was the only alcohol I ever saw you drink.'

'It's the only wine I like,' she said, smiling a little.

The waiter removed the cork with the minimum of fuss and poured. Nick picked up his glass, looked at her with eyes of polished gold, and said, 'Here's to success.'

Cat repeated the phrase, wondering sardonically what success he meant. Champagne slid cleanly across her tongue, cool and dry, the bubbles prickling deliciously.

Nick waited until she set the glass down to say, 'You'll need new clothes, and a ring.'

'What?'

He gave her a narrow smile. 'Not an engagement ring, but something big and expensive enough to mean business, and I think you should wear it on your engagement finger.'

She bit her lip, and he finished negligently, 'You can keep it when this is over.'

'I don't want it,' she retorted with crisp precision.

'You haven't seen it yet.'

'Have you?' Stupid question—when had Nick left anything to chance?

'Yes. It matches your eyes.' This time his smile held more than a hint of irony. 'We'll pick it up after lunch.'

Cat's appetite fled, but Nick began to talk of the yacht race series, and by the time her smoked chicken salad arrived her nerves had settled down enough for her to hold up her end in the conversation.

Glen had told her that Nick had been a handsome young savage, but there were no signs of uncouthness now in the man her husband had mentored. Natural intelligence, refined by the best education Glen had been able to provide and Nick's own ferocious determination, had polished away the rough edges.

'I don't need new clothes,' she said halfway through the meal. 'I still have some decent ones.'

His fingers tightened around the champagne flute. 'They'll be out of date,' he said pleasantly. 'Francesca would notice. Think of it as buying a uniform.'

She didn't want him paying for her clothes. When she remained silent, he added with a flicker of scorn, 'If you're worrying about money, I'm picking up the tab.'

'It just doesn't seem necessary,' she said lamely.

His guarded eyes scanned her face. 'It's necessary to me,' he said without emphasis. 'Preparation is all-important, and so is covering all the bases.'

Clearly he wasn't going to give in. 'I'll pay you back when I get a job,' she said with determination, and added, 'Has it occurred to you that Francesca might not care that you have a supposedly live-in lover? Some women don't—it only makes them more determined.'

'I expect you to make it obvious that you're the woman in possession,' he said calmly. 'I'll back you up. And I know that you can be just as determined as she is.'

When Cat refused to rise to the bait, he changed the subject. 'Which boutique did you buy your clothes from?'

Uncomfortably, she said, 'I liked Pan best.'

'All right,' he said, as though he'd done this plenty of times, 'we'll go there after this.'

Cat blinked when he came into the discreet shop with her. The owner greeted her with an enthusiasm that wasn't faked and took due note of the man with her.

When he said, 'I'll pick you up in a couple of hours, Cat,' she nodded and smiled, wondering what one did now.

He bent and dropped a swift, hard kiss on her mouth, before saying to the owner, 'You'll need an imprint of my credit card.'

'Certainly; come this way,' she said, smiling.

So that was how men paid for their mistress's clothes. Touched by a sleazy finger-stroke of degradation, Cat turned away to survey a draped length of scarlet satin above a tall black urn.

When Nick had left the owner observed, 'Not your colour—not with that gorgeous chestnut hair. I've got something that will do far better than that—a glorious little slip frock in just that glowing red-brown.'

Cat said awkwardly, 'I really don't need much—it's mainly for the Dempster Cup festivities.'

'I know exactly what you need,' the older woman said cheerfully. 'Half of Auckland's already been in—the half that doesn't buy in Australia or Paris—but as it happens I have a new shipment, and you're going to look wonderful in some of the garments.'

Cat chose carefully, buying sports clothes that weren't going to be of any use to her in her professional career, and two evening outfits. The exclusive shoe shop next door sent in an assistant with a selection of footwear, and she chose some to match the chic clothes—little sandals, casual boat shoes, timeless courts.

'You've changed,' the owner said when at last the decisions had been made. 'You're much more confident now, and you've developed your own style.'

'Thank you.'

The door swung open and Nick strode in; he smiled at Cat and she went white, the breath suddenly sucked from her lungs. Something uncompromising and powerful glinted in his eyes; oh, she fumed, he knew exactly the effect he had on her.

Because she had the same effect on him, she reminded herself, but that sounded very much like clinging to straws.

'Finished?' he asked without expression, although a faint raw note roughened his voice.

'Yes, thank you.'

'When will they be ready?'

The boutique owner said cheerfully, 'You can take them now. Lucky for her, she's a perfect petite size—nothing needed alteration.'

His glance at Cat lingered, amused and possessive. Cat thought she heard the owner of the shop sigh.

'Then let's go,' he said.

This time the car was a large saloon with a driver. Middle-aged, he leapt out when they approached, held the door open and took the parcels from Nick, who gave him an address before following Cat into the back and asking, 'When can you finish working in that restaurant?'

'Andreo's daughter comes home shortly.'

He frowned. 'So it's only a temporary job?'

'Yes.'

'Can you get off earlier?'

She shook her head. 'I promised him I'd stay until then.' And she needed the money.

Nick didn't look satisfied. 'What are you doing to find a position?'

'I've sent my CV out everywhere,' she told him, 'but no one's interested until I get confirmation of my degree. Besides, the holidays are coming up.'

He nodded, and they discussed her prospects like two acquaintances—if you ignored the crackle of awareness between them. Nick made some intelligent suggestions, and she was scribbling down several of them in her diary when the car drew up outside a building in one of the inner-city backstreets.

Once out, Nick took her elbow and escorted her into the narrow, anonymous foyer. Two flights up, and after what seemed excessive security precautions, they arrived in the showroom of a manufacturing jeweller.

Cat looked around with an interest that soon became respect and admiration. The designer had a distinctive mood and touch that appealed enormously to her, although none of the pieces, she noted, had a price.

'Nick!'

Cat flinched, her first wild thought one of betrayal, because the woman who came through the door from the back was the one he'd been talking to outside the restaurant. She glanced up at Nick, catching a glimpse of anger in the opaque depths of his eyes. Tension strung her nerves on wires as he introduced them.

'Catherine, this is Morna Vause, an old friend of mine.'

Cat offered her hand, but Morna had already turned away. Feeling foolish, she let it drop to her side.

'The ring's right here,' Morna said with a quick glance

over her shoulder. She unlocked a safe and drew out a jewel box, setting it down on the counter as she looked at Cat. In a voice that held a subliminal challenge, she said, 'Nick and I grew up together—lived next door to each other in the worst street in Auckland. It's thanks to him that I got away. He's the sort of big brother every woman should have.'

If that was meant to be reassuring, she'd got it wrong, Cat thought tautly. Something very odd was going on here. Was Morna Vause a discarded lover? No, Nick wouldn't be so crass. Morna must belong to the family who'd taken him in when things got too bad at home. She looked to be about the same age as Nick.

When Morna leaned forward to peer into Cat's eyes, Cat endured that comprehensive stare with gritted teeth, relieved when the older woman drew back and said, 'Yes, you were right, Nick. Almost exactly the same colour. Now, if you'll both excuse me, I'm on the phone in the office, so I'll go and finish my call.'

She disappeared. Nick's long fingers flipped back the lid of the box; inside glowed a ring set with a stone unlike any Cat had seen before. Purple-blue as the essence of summer sky and sea, it glittered in a setting of spiralling diamonds, delicate yet not fragile.

Nick plucked the ring from the white satin and slowly Cat held out her hand. He slid it onto her finger, settling it there, holding it until the gold warmed beneath his grip.

'Look at me,' he said beneath his breath.

Startled, she looked up, and his hard mouth curved in a twisted smile. 'We'd better do what Morna expects us to,' he said, and bent his head.

It was pure seeking; he took her lips in a demanding, possessive kiss that sent her senses reeling. Cat didn't think of resisting him; she didn't think at all.

When he lifted his head she stared into eyes so intense and keen that she thought they could see right through her frail façade of confidence.

What have I done? she thought, panicking as her body thrummed with desire.

'It suits you,' Nick said in a voice that echoed through her body. 'Rare and unusual.' He lifted her hand to his mouth and kissed the ring, then turned her hand over and pressed his mouth to the mound beneath her thumb.

Cat dragged in a harsh, shuddering breath that transmuted into a shocked gasp. Something wild and erotic flashed through her at the touch of his teeth on her skin. She jerked her hand free and stared at him with widening eyes before she looked down at the ring and asked in an unsteady voice, 'What is the stone? Is it a sapphire?'

'Tanzanite,' he said calmly.

The soft noise of a door opening and closing brought Cat's head up. She expected Nick to move away, but he stayed close—too close for the nerves jangling inside her.

Morna said, 'They've only ever been found in one mine in Tanzania, and I believe it's flooded now. A stone like that—perfect, and such a magnificent colour—is really rare.' She looked at Cat with veiled curiosity. 'Do you like it?'

Cat said, 'It's utterly beautiful.'

Eyes flicking up to Nick's unreadable face, Morna laughed. 'I think she likes it.'

His voice was cool and ironic. 'I'm sure she does. You've done a brilliant job.'

Morna's mouth moved in an odd smile, but she said in a professional tone, 'Anything for you, Nick. And that's a fabulous stone. It looks wonderful on your hand, Catherine—Nick said it would when he chose it. But you already know he's got terrific taste.'

'Thank you,' Nick said, a note of warning underlying the conventional phrase.

Morna shrugged, her gaze returning to Cat's face. 'Think nothing of it.'

Back in the car, Cat stared at the ring. 'Why didn't you ask her to do this for you?'

'Do what?'

On a flare of anger she said, 'You know what I mean. Pretend to be your lover.'

He leaned back into the seat and looked straight ahead. 'Because she and I don't want each other sexually,' he said bluntly. 'We grew up as if we were brother and sister, and it would show.' He turned his head and surveyed her with molten eyes.

Cat's heart jumped in her body. Hands clenching on her knees, she watched the stone flash in a shaft of sunlight, and said thickly, 'It's a crazy idea.'

'Come up with a better one.'

She bit her lip because of course she couldn't. So she muttered, 'This ring is too personal.'

Nick's brows drew together. 'Engagement rings...or the rings one gives to one's lover as a token of appreciation,' he said blandly, 'are very personal.'

Cat cast around for words to tell him what she meant, but had to be content with, 'Diamonds would have been more appropriate.'

Even to her it sounded lame; however, she wasn't going to say that this ring, with its false promise of love and intimacy, hurt her more than his cruel words could.

When he didn't reply she looked up and saw that he was still frowning, his angular profile sculpted against the hurrying crowds in the street. Trying hard to distract herself from the slow, sweet heat in the pit of her stomach, Cat thought that it took only one warm, languorous day for

Aucklanders to break out the colourful clothes of summer, linens and silks and cottons.

'On the "diamonds are a girl's best friend" theory? Or because they're conventional and therefore safe? I want it to be obvious that everything about our relationship is extremely personal,' Nick said, turning his head to catch her looking at him. His heavy lids drooped. 'Francesca is every bit as astute as you are, and she's just as capable of reading nuances. To fool her, we need something much more intense than the usual light affair. We may not be engaged, but we are definitely obsessed with each other—to the extent that any intervention on her part is going to be useless.'

Chilled, Cat asked tartly, 'Obsessed? What happened to love?'

An ironic smile twisted his mouth. 'I think Francesca believes in love as much as I do,' he said, adding smoothly, 'As much as you do, Cat. Love is for innocents who still believe in romance and living happily ever after.'

Repressing a shiver, she turned her hand slightly so that the light collected and pooled and flashed. 'I'm not going to sleep in the same room as you,' she said bluntly.

'I haven't suggested it.'

His equable answer left her breathless and irritated yet determined. 'So where *will* I sleep?' she asked.

'My house has a master suite. The private sitting room can be converted into another bedroom.' Lean, tanned fingers enclosed her restless hands, holding them still. 'There are even two bathrooms,' he said, 'so you won't have to worry about coming across me in the shower.'

Could he feel her jumping pulses? Possibly, but he wouldn't know that deep inside she was melting, her whole body afire with need and a bitter ache of passion. Cautiously she tried to tug her hands free, but his tightened around them, keeping them prisoner.

Huskily she said, 'I thought you lived in the apartment.'

'I use it as a *pied-à-terre*, somewhere to stay when I'm in Auckland, but my real home is north of Auckland.' He lifted her hands to his mouth, kissing the palm of one and then the other.

Cat flinched at the amusement and an arrogant satisfaction that flared in the golden depths of his eyes before he put her hands back in her lap. He knew he possessed the power to make her witless and weak with hunger for him, and he'd use that power if he had to.

It humiliated her to admit it, but he could strip her of confidence, of everything she'd fought to acquire, and send her naked and shivering into the world.

She said curtly, 'No, I'm not going to do it.'

'Spoken like a true coward,' he said, his voice laced with contempt. He leaned back into his seat and scrutinised her. 'I thought it wouldn't be long before your concern for that poor little scrap in Romit wore thin.' When she glared mutely at him he asked with steel running through his tone, 'What exactly did you want the money for, Cat?'

'What a suspicious mind you have,' she hurled, guilty because for a moment she'd forgotten Juana.

'Answer me.'

The flinty, implacable note in his voice reminded her that, as well as intelligence and dynamism, he'd used ruthlessness to reach the position he'd achieved.

Something Glen had once said flashed into her mind. 'Beneath that sophisticated surface, Nick will always be a savage, hard and compelling and uncompromising. It's his greatest asset and his biggest drawback.'

She suspected she was seeing the savage now, and she lifted her head proudly. 'What do you think I might need it for?'

'Oh, there are quite a few things you could do with twenty thousand dollars…pay bills, buy drugs…'

'What?'

His eyes had narrowed into slivers of pure, intense gold, hypnotic, compelling. 'Is that it?'

'No,' she said stonily, fighting a fierce, obscure disappointment because he still suspected her. 'The only drugs I ever take are prescribed by a doctor. You can stop this car now and let me out.'

She looked towards the driver, but it was obvious that he hadn't heard her through the transparent partition.

Beside her she heard Nick laugh quietly. 'Imperious as ever,' he said. 'All right, I believe you. So tell me why you suddenly changed your mind.'

Of course she couldn't. Once he realised how defenceless she was against her own weakness he'd probably see no reason not to take her.

'It's deceitful and distasteful,' she said harshly. She glanced down at the ring. 'I'm sure your friend will take this back.'

'Oh, Morna would take it back,' he said casually. 'As for deceit—well, Francesca is tough and this is war.'

'She sounds awful.'

'Not at all; I like her,' he said. 'She's intelligent and entertaining and she knows what she wants, but she likes living dangerously. Unfortunately I don't want to marry her. We'd end up killing each other.'

His sudden, wicked grin took Cat by surprise. Hastily stopping herself from smiling back, she said, 'I hate telling lies.'

'You won't need to tell a single lie,' he said calmly.

'Act a lie, then.'

His brows rose. 'Make up your mind, Cat, yes or no.' And when she still hesitated, he said softly, 'Now.'

Juana, Cat thought heavily. She had to do this. And, refusing to face the thought that she was yielding partly because she couldn't bear the thought of him falling prey to a seductress, even one he liked—*especially* one he liked!—she said reluctantly, 'Juana has to have that operation as soon as possible.'

'I'll send half the money to the clinic immediately, and when the Barringtons go back to Australia I'll send the rest.'

She met his gaze. 'I want a contract. Or—well, something.'

After a moment of intimidating silence he said tonelessly, 'Of course. I'll have my lawyer draw it up.' He reached into his briefcase and took out a computer diary. After he'd made a note into it, he said, 'You can come to lunch with me tomorrow and see it.'

Feeling as though she'd crushed something so newborn it hadn't had time to form, Cat pulled the ring off her finger and held it out. 'You'd better look after this.'

He nodded and took it, slipping it into the breast pocket of his superbly cut suit. 'All right.'

They didn't exchange any more conversation until the car drew up beside her house.

Nick got out before the driver could and opened the door for her, looking down at her with an expressionless face. 'I'll send the car to pick you up tomorrow at midday,' he said.

Cat nodded. 'Thank you very much for lunch,' she said politely. 'It was delicious.'

'Thank you,' he returned with an equal courtesy so remote it was a rebuff.

Cat turned and walked away from the car, into the house and up the stairs.

She changed into jeans and a T-shirt and wandered

around the room before sitting down at her desk. Aimlessly she hefted a textbook and read its name aloud. She put it back and leaned forward with her elbows on the desk, cupping her face in her hands.

Glen hadn't wanted her to go to university. He'd argued and quarrelled with her, forbidden it, only arriving at a sullen acceptance when he'd realised that he couldn't stop her. And even then he'd conducted guerilla warfare against her decision, making it difficult for her to study.

When her mother had asked her why it was so necessary to upset him she hadn't been able to answer, hadn't even known why she wanted so much to take a degree.

She understood now; she'd used her studies to take her mind off the mistake she'd made in marrying him.

Now she was confronted with an even bigger mistake—and she must never forget that although Nick wanted her, he despised her.

CHAPTER FIVE

WHEN the car arrived the next day, Cat had spent an hour deciding what to wear, finally choosing a pair of narrow trousers. She topped them with a Chinese-style silk blouse she'd found in the markets at Ilid before the rebellion.

Not entirely suitable for lunch at a restaurant, but it was all she had apart from her blue suit, and she wasn't wearing that again.

Dissatisfied, she peered at her reflection, a little mollified by the way the moody blues and greens of the blouse emphasised her eyes and the clarity of her skin.

Not that it mattered, because the last thing she wanted to do was appeal to the sensualist in Nick. That just complicated things; unless they could bypass this naked, barely restrainable hunger and achieve some sort of closure, some settlement of the past, they'd always be caught in a tangle of turbulent, unsatisfied passion and guilt.

Ignoring the niggle of panic beneath her breastbone, she picked up her bag and ran down to the car.

The driver, his weather-beaten face made interesting by a pair of remarkably shrewd eyes, wished her good afternoon, opened the rear door and closed it behind her. The solid thunk sounded like the slamming of a prison door.

Oh, for heaven's sake, she commanded, stop dramatising! After fastening the seatbelt she leaned back and deliberately relaxed her facial muscles.

But a few minutes later she looked at the harbour bridge in astonishment. Were they going to eat on the North Shore...?

No, the car forged steadily along the motorway, heading away from Auckland.

After a couple of minutes Cat fathomed how to work the communications system. 'Excuse me,' she said into it, 'where exactly are we going?'

The driver said formally, 'Up to Nick's—Mr Harding's house, madam.'

'Oh.' Feeling foolish, she said, 'I hadn't realised.'

'I'm sorry, madam; I thought you knew.'

'It's all right.' She hesitated, then said, 'And please don't call me madam. I'm not used to it.'

All he said was, 'Very well,' but she could hear a grin in his voice.

Satisfied, she leaned back and looked warily out of the windows. Perhaps Nick had told her; no, she'd have remembered. She remembered everything he'd said in that deep voice with its fascinating, abrasive thread twining around each word.

No doubt he wanted to show her the house she was supposed to be sharing with him.

Temporarily, she reminded herself sternly, repressing the involuntary leap in her heart.

So suddenly she didn't realise what was happening, she slid into sleep.

Nick had spent the morning working in his office, and planned to stay there while Rob brought Cat inside, but when he heard the rattle of wheels over the cattlestop he abandoned the agreement he'd got his lawyer to draw up overnight, and walked out through the wide front door.

Grinning, Rob cut the engine and put a finger across his lips before he opened his door and got out. Nick's eyes narrowed; he stared through the darkened windows into the back of the car and saw Cat's bright head lolling sideways.

An odd constriction in his chest strangling his breath, he took the two steps down to the drive fast and clumsily.

'She fell asleep before we got off the motorway,' Rob murmured, taking care not to slam his door.

Nick found he could breathe again. Cat's slender body had slumped, but even in sleep she couldn't be anything but graceful and provocative. He'd give a lot to see her like that in his bed, he thought, fighting to control the obstinate hunger prowling through him. He knew he was heading into dangerous waters, but, damn it, he wanted her as he'd never wanted another woman.

And she was just as vulnerable as he was; whenever they touched she responded with a reciprocal passion that hardened his body as he remembered the slumbrous eyes, the fiery desire in her kisses.

They'd set the world on fire.

But when the fire had died to ashes, would they at last be able to get on with their lives? Because these past two years had just been marking time, he acknowledged reluctantly. No, make that six years—ever since he'd seen her with Glen's engagement ring on her finger.

Quietly, he unlatched the door and leaned in to unclip her safety belt.

The prowling, seething frustration he'd repressed for years had to be what fed this forbidden obsession, so when his hunger had been sated of course he'd be free of her. Naturally he'd see that she had a decent job; none of this working nights in backstreet restaurants. He knew just what strings to pull, and once he had her settled, surely he'd be able to prise her out of his mind.

She didn't stir, so he slid his arms around her and lifted her out. She fitted as though made for his embrace only, her slender body relaxing against him so lightly he could straighten up without taking a deeper breath.

Forgetting everything else, he absorbed her—the straight, fine chestnut hair gleaming in the sun, her pale, translucent skin, flushed and warm, the long-lashed eyelids that covered her exotic, smoky, seductive eyes...eyes that promised everything, that held secrets in their clear depths.

He could, he thought with savage anger, stand like this for the rest of the afternoon, just holding her.

A small movement broke the spell; he looked across Cat's head into the eyes of his driver. Expressionlessly Rob said, 'I'll bring her bag in.'

'Thank you.' Nick set off for the house, torn by a feral mixture of fury and violent desire.

Cat's mouth tightened, then smoothed out into a half-smile as she muttered something.

Sheer, stark jealousy jolted through him. Had she said 'Glen'? No—it had been a slow, huskily questioning syllable, the sound a woman might make when she woke in a man's arms.

Schooling his voice into an amusement that didn't quite hide a much more elemental roughness, Nick said, 'Cat.'

Blindly she turned her head and burrowed into his chest. The childish little movement summoned a shocked tenderness, followed by a kind of fear. Subduing it—for what had he to fear from her?—he said abruptly, 'Cat! Come on, it's time to wake up.'

Another of those seductive, indeterminate noises reached his ears, and then she woke properly, fixing him with a gaze as mysterious and depthless as the evening sky.

He saw the moment she recognised him, the swift fall of her lashes and the instinctive stiffening of her slight body.

Cat wanted to die. His strength enfolded her, surrounding her with the faint, disturbing scent that belonged only to Nick, and a masculine heat that sapped her of energy and robbed her brain of anything but a witless, seeking response as involuntary as it was primal.

Rigid with embarrassment, she said in a choked voice, 'I'm awake. You can put me down now.'

His mouth twisted with mocking amusement, he set her on the ground, keeping his arm around her when her legs wouldn't hold her up. Salvation came in the guise of the driver, coming up behind with her handbag.

She found a smile somewhere and directed it to him. 'Thank you,' she croaked. 'I'll bet you don't often have people treating your car like a bedroom.'

The driver grinned back at her, and offered her the bag. 'Must mean I'm a good driver,' he said cheerfully.

Nick's arm tightened a moment around her shoulders, then dropped away. 'You look,' he said after a narrowed survey, 'rather fragile. Have you been up all night?'

A fugitive colour tinged Cat's skin. Forcing her tired brain to think, she hedged, 'I went to bed just after midnight.'

But she'd barely slept—and the previous night had been wakeful too.

'You need a drink and some lunch,' Nick said, urging her around and up the steps. 'Welcome to my home.'

Quickly, nervously, she said, 'I don't know why, but I thought you lived on the coast.'

Instead the house overlooked a twenty-kilometre spread of fertile farmland and bush, terminated by a range of blue hills on the horizon. The long, modern building, many-windowed and beautiful, had been built on several levels, and was sheltered from cold southerly winds by the bush-clad hill rising behind.

Although *bush*, Cat thought now as she assessed Nick's land, was an inadequate word to describe the splendid rain-forest that brooded over the valley.

This place was a glimpse into Nick's dreams. Completely satisfying to the eye, in some subtle way the house matched his powerful, complex character. Set in magnificent young gardens, and buffered by paddocks where cattle and several horses grazed, the whole property was like a fantasy of pastoral life, all serenity and grace.

Could Nick be thinking dynastically, planning for a wife to manage the house and help him fill it with children? Sudden pain slashed across Cat's self-possession.

'I intended to buy on the coast,' he said, 'but when I saw this I knew it was what I really wanted.'

Cat drew a shaky breath and pretended to examine the wide tiled entryway, the graceful, spacious proportions of the house. 'It's beautiful,' she said in a muted voice, gripped by an odd feeling of rightness, of homecoming, a recognition so intense that it almost hurt.

She'd never felt anything like it before.

Oh, yes, you have, memory warned her inconveniently. The first time you saw Nick.

The huge door opened onto a hall floored in the same warm Italian tiles as the steps and the entryway; sunlight poured in, illuminating a magnificent photograph of the valley that hung on one wall.

'I had a good architect,' he said. 'Philip Angove.'

It was a name she knew, but although Philip Angove—who only designed houses for people he liked—was world-famous, Cat's glance glimmered with disbelief as she said, 'I imagine you told him exactly what you wanted.'

Nick lifted his brows. 'You know me so well.' The flicker of amusement had vanished from his dark face, leaving it cold and arrogantly uncompromising.

Was he remembering her accusation that he knew nothing about her?

Hastily she walked across to stand in front of the photograph on the wall. Closer inspection revealed that it wasn't a photograph but an oil painting. When something about the technique looked familiar she peered more closely, remembering the nude on his office wall, the woman with hair the same colour as hers. 'Who's the artist?' she asked.

He told her the name. 'He paints reality and then distorts it,' he said.

She looked again at the painting, and, sure enough, although superficially a super-realistic view of the valley, closer inspection revealed a castle, dark and forbidding, where the house stood. On the ramparts stood two people, a tall man in armour and a cloaked woman.

Shivers scudded down her spine.

'Would you like a shower before we eat?' Nick asked with remote courtesy.

She shook her head. 'No, thank you, but I'd like to wash my face. It feels creased.'

Something gleamed in the amber depths of his eyes. 'It looks like gently crumpled satin. There's a powder room along this way.'

Once safely inside, Cat glanced around a room of austere luxury before washing her face and combing her hair into order, then reapplying lipstick. With the fragile gloss of her confidence burnished, she emerged to find Nick walking in through the front door. Bright sunlight threw into relief his lean body, moving with the prowling awareness of a predator, every long muscle coiled for instant action.

Honed by his presence, Cat's senses sprang to full alert. An unaccustomed recklessness fizzed through her, seductive, dangerous.

'Barricades back in place?' he said, an ironic smile not softening his mouth. Without waiting for an answer, he said, 'It's warm enough to eat outside so Mrs Hannay's set the table in the sunken garden.'

Behind the house a terrace stretched across to a swimming pool. On its furthest side water fell in a straight curtain down a wall and into a sunken garden where a table and chairs sheltered in the shade.

Descending a wide, shallow flight of steps, Cat gazed around, her eyes dazzled by the unexpectedness of the hidden garden. 'You'd never know there was a gully here. From the front it looks as though the hill stretches up behind the house without any interruption.'

'It wasn't a natural watercourse—nobody knows who dug out a pit here last century, or why, but I suspect it had something to do with felling kauri trees. I was going to fill it with the swimming pool, but the woman who designed the garden—'

'I'll bet it was Perdita Dennison! She does great things with water,' Cat interrupted, wondering what Nick had thought of the tall, beautiful, ex-supermodel. Still, Perdita and her husband Luke were notorious for their happy marriage.

'She persuaded me to do this and put the pool up closer to the house.' He looked around at the clever, intricate design of walls that formed plant boxes as they rose to the sunlit wilderness of the rainforest behind the house. 'I thought it should be a wild garden, and when she suggested gardenias and cycads and clipped jasmine so close to the bush I thought she was crazy, but she's good. It works.'

'She's more than good, she's brilliant.' At the bottom of the steps Cat stopped to look around with frank pleasure. 'She uses plants so cleverly—who'd have thought of blending a Mediterranean garden into nikau palms and tree ferns? But it's perfect. And I love the citrus trees, and the way the oranges echo the colour of the terracotta pots.'

'You sound as though you like gardens,' Nick said, watching her with half-closed eyes.

She shrugged. 'I suppose I absorbed an affection for them by osmosis—my father loved to garden.'

Nick asked, 'How did he die, Cat?'

She dipped her fingers into a narrow tiled channel that collected the softly falling water from the pool and directed it around two sides of the sunken paved floor.

Looking down at her wet hand, she said, 'It was a stupid, useless accident. He was driving along the road and a neighbour on a tractor came hurtling out of a driveway. Dad hadn't heard him because a truck was going past. He hadn't heard Dad for the same reason. The impact pushed Dad's car into the truck.'

'Tough,' Nick said. Only a monosyllable, yet she sensed sympathy. 'Your mother told me once that you blamed yourself for it.'

Cat shook her hand, watching the drops of water flick across the tiles. 'I'd forgotten to get cumin seeds for a dish I wanted to make for dinner that night. I was being a drama queen about it, so he rushed off into town to get some for me.'

Perfume from the white flowers on low-growing hedges of gardenias mingled in the warm air with the fresh, mysterious fragrance of the bush, and the stiff, palm-like cycads gave an exotic, primeval look to the garden. Somehow the sight and sound and scent of it soothed an ache of grief she'd never been able to forget.

Nick said uncompromisingly, 'You can't blame yourself for that.'

'It's not logical, is it?' She lifted unseeing eyes. 'But I'm not very logical.' More drops of water fell from her fingers onto the tiles.

'And then you met Glen,' Nick said neutrally.

She nodded.

'Where and how?' he asked.

A wide, tiled bench ran around three parts of the garden. Cat eased herself down onto it and looked across into the shady area where someone had set a long table with two places. 'I backed into his car in the supermarket car park,' she admitted. 'He took me home because I kept bursting into tears.' She paused, then added defiantly, 'He was very kind.'

'I see.' Nick spoke with no expression, but there was no kindness in his words.

She said tautly, 'Perdita Dennison is a magician. This garden looks like you.'

'I'm flattered,' Nick said, almost bored, gesturing at the table. 'Come and sit down and we can eat. How does it look like me?'

Colour stung her skin. On a challenging note she said, 'Sophistication and control married to a secret, subliminal wildness.'

Interrupted only by the low hum of bees, silence stretched between them until it was broken by Nick in a tone that stung like a whip.

'That's an interesting summing-up of my character. I didn't realise you agreed with those silly women who believe that because I grew up in one of the poorer suburbs I'm not entirely civilised.' His tone emphasised his distaste. 'Some even see it as sexually exciting. I must be a disappointment to them.'

Shocked to discover that her main emotion was a ferocious protectiveness that had come out of nowhere, Cat lifted her chin and said sturdily, 'They're stupid, and I'm not going to make any more assumptions, although if you agreed to the plans for this, it must appeal to you.'

'Perhaps I wanted to prove myself—or show off,' he suggested, pulling back a chair and holding it in place.

Unrestrained laughter rippled from her. Sliding into the chair, she said, 'You? Nick Harding? You don't care what anyone thinks of you, and you've already proved yourself in every way that counts.'

'Ah—materially,' he said with smooth sarcasm, sitting down opposite her.

She said fiercely, 'That too, but you fulfilled Glen's faith in you, and your own confidence in your ability.'

There followed another of those silences, but this one had something ominous in it. After a tense moment Cat looked away from the hot gold of Nick's scrutiny to concentrate on the tabletop, so dark a blue it was almost black. On it, simple white dishes and a bunch of yellow and white daisies in a green glass jug glowed in the midday light, and stray sunbeams winked off knives and forks.

It looked, she thought derisively, like a setting from a good magazine—country casual, country smart, but with an underlying sophistication that somehow didn't sit oddly with the primeval lushness of the bush.

To Cat's relief a woman appeared at the top of the steps with a tray. Nick strode up to take it from her, and when they'd both reached the bottom of the flight he introduced her. Small, square, about forty, with eyebrows that met above her nose, a determined chin and a surprisingly sweet smile, she was Mrs Hannay, Nick's housekeeper.

The food she set in front of them ravished Cat's tastebuds as effectively as the house and garden pleased her eyes—a green, green soup made of spinach, sparked with blue cheese and nutmeg.

After several mouthfuls Cat said with delicate greed, 'This is delicious!' She crunched into a toasted slice of French bread. 'You're so lucky. Inspired cooks are rare.'

Before they'd begun to eat Nick had asked if she'd wanted wine, but she'd refused, intrigued to see that one of the walls hid a built-in alcove that contained glasses and a fridge.

'The party cupboard,' Nick said, pouring them both chilled mineral water. 'It saves Mrs Hannay from running up and down the steps.'

Cat picked up the glass and drank. 'Everything's so green here,' she said quietly. 'In Romit it was dry and dusty and hot, and then the monsoon came and it was wet and muddy and hot.'

'Did you see any fighting?'

When she hesitated he said harshly, 'Tell me the truth.'

'Not fighting exactly,' she evaded. 'A couple of raids, that's all.'

'Were you hurt?'

'The locals told us when they were coming, and we hid. The peacekeeping force moved onto the island before the main body of insurgents had a chance to reach our area, but we had refugees, and some soldiers were brought to the clinic by relatives.' Many had died of their wounds.

Although his face remained expressionless a muscle beat in his jaw and his voice was low and angry. 'Why didn't you get out when your friend and her father left? Talk about foolhardy courage! It was crazy to stay—God knows what might have happened to you if the world hadn't suddenly made up its mind that enough was enough.'

'I didn't stay because I was crazy or courageous, or even because I felt I might be able to help. By then Juana had been born—I couldn't abandon her.'

Heavy lashes screened his eyes so that she couldn't see what he was thinking—not, she thought bitterly, that she ever could. He said bluntly, 'Even though you put yourself—and the clinic—in danger?'

She bit her lip, because she'd realised too late that her presence was a constant worry for the harried nuns at the clinic and the terrified locals. 'She was my responsibility,' she reiterated stubbornly.

He evidently felt he'd made his point because he changed the subject, telling her about a meeting he'd been at the previous afternoon with a man known for his eccentricities.

Long before they'd finished their soup, Nick's dry, not unkind humour made her laugh, and kept her laughing throughout the meal. He was, she found herself thinking as dizzily as though the mineral water had been champagne, the best of companions—stimulating, provocative, so that her mind raced to keep up with his.

When lunch was over and Mrs Hannay had cleared the table, Cat got to her feet and stood looking up into the mysterious, sun-splashed depths of the bush, sorry that this enchanted hour was gone; instinct warned her that it had been a precious time out of time.

From behind Nick said without preamble, 'There's been a change of plan; you'll be moving in tomorrow.'

She swivelled to stare at his formidable face. 'I can't possibly! My job at the restaurant—'

'You've worked your last night there,' he said on an implacable note.

She said sharply, 'Lending me money doesn't mean you can order me around like someone you've bought.'

His smile was slow and cruel. 'I didn't realise it was a loan. I thought I had bought you,' he said silkily, and laughed at the sudden anger in her face.

'In your dreams!' Her pulse drummed in her ears. 'I'll pay you back as soon as I can.'

A swift flush of colour along his gypsyish cheekbones made her wonder if he was going to lose his temper. The colour faded almost as soon as it came, and he said coldly, 'I don't want your money. The contract you insisted on states that your assistance with this—project—negates any debt you might owe me. But I decide when you start and when you finish. You start now.'

She paused, reining back the hot words that trembled on her tongue. He didn't have to directly threaten her; if she didn't agree, Juana would have to wait for her operation.

His broad shoulders moved as though he'd flexed them to rid himself of tightness. 'I've rung Andreo and told him you won't be coming back.'

'Then you can just ring him again and tell him you made a mistake!'

'I've organised another waitress to work there in your place,' Nick said inflexibly.

Cat glared at him. 'He won't *need* another waitress, because I'll be there.'

'You're going to work yourself into exhaustion. Sleeping in the car—'

'I went to sleep because I—' Hot-faced, she bit the words back. No way was she going to tell him that she'd been tired because she'd spent the night fantasising about him. Instead she swung off onto another tangent. 'Agreeing to this crazy plan doesn't give you the right to take over my life, do you hear? I haven't signed that contract yet. You had no right to go behind my back.'

Mrs Hannay appeared at the top of the steps that led up to the house. As though she hadn't just walked out into a violent spat, she said, 'Call for you, Nick. Will you take it here, or in the house?'

His eyes still on Cat's angry face, he said formally, 'Excuse me,' and left her.

Fuming, Cat walked up the steps and around to the border of garden and rainforest. She stopped in the shade, her eyes roving the lacy pinwheels of the treeferns while her heart settled down to a more even pace. Who the hell did Nick think he was, ordering her life to suit himself…?

Yet for Juana's sake she had to endure this bitter servitude.

Slowly, subtly, the soft clicking of the palm fronds in the whispering breeze soothed the tight knot of anger in her chest.

She was examining the delicate, pale pink flowers of a rose that had pretensions to taking over the world when Nick said abruptly from behind her, 'You're right. I should have consulted you first.'

For the second time her mouth dropped. Straightening up and turning, she said suspiciously, 'Then you'll tell Andreo that I'll be back?,'

'No,' he said with cool arrogance, 'because that was a call from Francesca Barrington. She and her father are arriving tomorrow, and since their yacht won't be here for another four days they'll be staying here with me. With us. I want you on my arm and doing a creditable performance as the woman in possession when they arrive.'

CHAPTER SIX

'TOMORROW?' Cat exclaimed, her heart skidding too heavily in her chest.

Nick was watching her with a narrowed stare, intense as a laser. 'Thinking of reneging on our deal, Cat?' he asked dangerously.

'No,' she said, searching for straws to cling to, and finding none. 'But I want to see that contract,' she finished desperately.

'Come on up and look at it now,' he said, reining in his impatience. 'Once we've agreed on it I'll take you home and help you pack.'

'Nobody packs my things but me,' she retorted, masking her surrender with crisp irritation. 'I'm surprised you can afford to take the time off.'

His swift grin took her by surprise again, sizzling through her. 'I work a lot from home,' he said. 'Let's go.'

It was like being taken over by a whirlwind. Half an hour later she was with him in the car, contract signed and stored away in his safe, wondering why she hadn't told him to get himself out of this situation—and wondering, after a resentful look at his determined jaw, why he couldn't freeze Francesca Barrington off without going to all this trouble.

Well, of course he could if he wanted to—if it weren't for business. Whatever deal he was working on with Stan Barrington meant a lot to him.

Nick, she thought wryly, wouldn't be Nick if he hadn't made sure he'd covered all the bases.

She'd read the contract with every ounce of acumen she

91

could summon, relieved that it was simple and to the point. In return for her assistance, involving staying at his house and accompanying him, he would pay her twenty thousand dollars, half now, half when the contract was completed.

Although she was completely determined to repay the money as a loan, she'd signed it, he'd signed it, and then he had telephoned his bank with instructions to forward ten thousand dollars to the clinic in Romit. A few minutes later the fax had chattered back with documentation showing that the amount had been transferred.

Very businesslike and impersonal.

But then, it all came back to business. Anyone Nick married—and judging by the women who flocked around him he was spoiled for choice—would soon learn that she was the secondary interest in his life. Like Glen, the cut and thrust, the sheer adrenalin charge of his work held more excitement for him than any woman.

No doubt the persistent Francesca thought she had the upper hand because she believed Nick needed either her father's money or his goodwill. Cat smiled ironically. Francesca would soon learn that it wasn't wise to try and back Nick into a corner.

And now Juana was halfway to the operation that would make such a difference to her life.

'Don't come up,' she said when the car turned into her street. 'I won't be long.'

'All right,' he said briefly after a measuring glance. 'I can work in the car. Come down and tell me when you're ready. Don't carry heavy suitcases down those stairs.'

'I won't.'

But as she heaved a suitcase out of her bedroom door one of the other students happened to be passing. 'Leaving us already?' he asked, eyeing the box of books she'd used to prop the door open.

'Hi, Linc.' She smiled at him.

'Here, I can take that down.'

'You don't need to...' But it would mean that Nick didn't see her grotty room. Honest poverty was all very well, but the thought of him pitying her lacerated her pride. 'That would be great, thanks.'

'A pleasure—I work out and get to impress you with my manly muscles at the same time as being useful,' Linc said cheerfully. 'Which is the heaviest?'

'The box of textbooks.'

He lifted it, then staggered elaborately back against the wall. 'They must be made from special, lead-impregnated paper. My spine may never be the same again.'

After poking a note beneath Sinead's door, Cat followed him, bumping her case down from stair to stair and abandoning it at the bottom while she ran ahead to open the door for her cavalier.

Nick was sitting in the car, black head bent over a folder of papers. When Cat appeared at the gate he looked up and got out to open the boot.

Linc gave a long, low moan. 'Oh, man, like, that's a *car*.'

Cat nodded. She'd probably never see the house again, she thought suddenly. In a few weeks there'd be nothing there but a neat, soulless parking lot. A sudden blast of colour caught her eye, and some of her sadness faded. Perhaps the house had had its day, but the daylilies would survive in the old lady's garden.

When the box had been dumped in the boot, she introduced Linc to Nick, who shook his hand and talked to him for a few minutes until the younger man said, 'I'd better go; I've got to get to work.' He turned to Cat. 'All the best,' he said, and before she realised what he was planning, he gave her an enthusiastic hug. 'You take care of yourself. I'm going to miss that stunning smile, you know, every time I have breakfast!'

The compliment warmed her. 'Good luck.' He felt young and gangly, unformed. On impulse, she stretched up and kissed his cheek. 'And say goodbye to the others for me, will you?'

'Will do,' he promised, looking pleased.

Nick waited until he was out of earshot before asking crisply, 'Where's the rest of your gear?'

'I've left my case at the bottom of the stairs,' she said.

'Stay here and I'll get it.'

Frowning, Cat watched him stride back up to the door. Something about the set of his shoulders and the way his long legs ate up the ground made her wonder what had made him angry.

She found out the next day when she saw Francesca Barrington, tall and glamorous, reach up and kiss him on the cheek.

Not that it was exactly anger—more like outrage that another woman should touch the man who belonged to her. And, although jealousy was a nasty, degrading emotion, Cat couldn't stop herself from gritting her teeth.

'You don't mind, I'm sure,' Francesca said to her, green eyes amused yet watchful. 'Nick and I are such old friends.'

'I don't mind in the least—Nick has so many old friends,' Cat said demurely. Although Francesca wasn't beautiful, she radiated something far more valuable than mere good looks—a vividness and vitality that made Cat feel pale and lifeless.

'I know, I know. Women draped around him like curtains.' Francesca glanced back at Nick. 'How long have you two known each other?'

'Six years,' Nick said casually. 'Where's Stan? I thought he was coming with you.'

Behind them Rob and the pilot were unloading suitcases from the helicopter.

Francesca's brows had shot up. 'Six years! You must have been a baby, Cathy.'

Nick had introduced her as Catherine; she disliked Cathy, but hated the possibility that Francesca might call her Cat. Only Nick called her that.

'Eighteen,' she said with a false air of composure. 'I thought I knew everything there was to know in the world.'

The other woman's eyes had narrowed, but this surprised a gurgle of laughter from her. 'Oh, I remember,' she said sympathetically, then looked up through her lashes at Nick. 'Dad couldn't come in the end—more dull old business, I'm afraid. He sent you his regards and said he'd see you when the yacht docks.'

Cat couldn't fault the tone or expression, but the older woman was, she thought with a flash of amusement, a worthy opponent for Nick!

'A pity,' he said easily. 'Let's go in, shall we?'

He tucked Cat's hand into his arm, and they all strolled through a gate into the garden.

'Goodness, how everything's grown!' Francesca said, gazing around. 'It's only a few months since I've been here, but what a difference! There can't be a better climate than New Zealand's for gardens.' She switched a glance to Cat. 'Are you a gardener?'

'Cat's an accountant,' Nick said, somehow infusing the bland answer with a warning note.

Francesca pulled a face. 'Can't accountants be gardeners? Perhaps not. I know it's a very worthwhile profession but it does suffer from an image problem.' Boring, her tone implied.

Cat smiled. 'Yes, but that's our cunning, you see. In a

short time we accountants plan to take over the world and no one will have seen it coming.'

She got a wide-eyed stare, followed by another amused gurgle before Francesca began to discuss the latest drop in the dollar.

As she showed Francesca her bedroom, Cat mentally thanked the architect for dividing the house so that the guest rooms were at the other end from what had probably been designated in the plans as the family sleeping area.

'Would you like someone to unpack for you?' Cat asked, feeling a total fraud. 'Dinner will be in an hour.'

Francesca shrugged. 'No, I know Nick doesn't have live-in maids. Don't worry, I can look after myself.' She smiled and disappeared into her room, closing the door behind her.

Oddly rebuffed, Cat walked briskly down the passage and into the room that was now hers.

The previous day, when Nick had taken her there, she'd looked around with something like despair. It was beautiful, a room that summoned dreams. The walls were a pale ivory, accent colours of gold and a smoky blue giving the room sophistication. A huge bed intensified the atmosphere with an elaborately carved headboard in some dark, exotic wood.

Wide, deep windows opened onto a private terrace shielded by foliage and walls from the rest of the garden. Cane chairs and an upholstered lounger provided a place to read or just to drowse. It had to be for reading, she'd decided; it was impossible to imagine Nick doing anything so lacking in energy as drowse in the sun!

Leading off the bedroom were two bathrooms and two dressing rooms, and on the other side was the sitting room that had been converted into a bedroom for Nick.

And *her* clothes were now hanging in one corner of the dressing room that had been allocated to her; *her* books

The Harlequin Reader Service® — Here's how it works:

If offer card is missing write to: Harlequin Reader Service, 3010 Walden Ave., P.O. Box 1867, Buffalo NY 14240-1867

NO POSTAGE
NECESSARY
IF MAILED
IN THE
UNITED STATES

BUSINESS REPLY MAIL
FIRST-CLASS MAIL   PERMIT NO. 717-003   BUFFALO, NY

POSTAGE WILL BE PAID BY ADDRESSEE

HARLEQUIN READER SERVICE
3010 WALDEN AVE
PO BOX 1867
BUFFALO NY 14240-9952

GET FREE BOOKS and a FREE GIFT WHEN YOU PLAY THE...

Lucky 7
SLOT MACHINE GAME!

Just scratch off the silver box with a coin. Then check below to see the gifts you get!

YES! I have scratched off the silver box. Please send me the 2 free Harlequin Presents® books and gift for which I qualify. I understand I am under no obligation to purchase any books, as explained on the back of this card.

306 HDL DRRK   **106 HDL DRRZ**

FIRST NAME   LAST NAME

ADDRESS

APT.#   CITY

STATE/PROV.   ZIP/POSTAL CODE

7	7	7	**Worth TWO FREE BOOKS plus a BONUS Mystery Gift!**
🍒	🍒	🍒	**Worth TWO FREE BOOKS!**
♣	♣	♣	**Worth ONE FREE BOOK!**
🔔	🔔	🍒	**TRY AGAIN!**

Visit us online at www.eHarlequin.com

(H-P-01/03)

DETACH AND MAIL CARD TODAY!

had been unpacked into the bookshelf; the elegant desk was covered with *her* far from elegant textbooks and notes—while she wondered what on earth she'd got herself into.

Romit and the clinic and Juana seemed far away from this luxurious house in its quiet countryside, from Francesca Barrington who breathed money and position, from Nick...

No, not from Nick. Oh, life in the mean streets of Auckland bore no resemblance to life on a war-torn island, but although the chances of him starving to death had been remote, he'd grown up in a war zone of sorts.

So in a way Nick was a link with Juana.

Cat walked across to the bedside table and opened the drawer into which she'd tumbled the contents of her bag, finding the only photograph she had of the baby. The luxurious room contrasted shockingly with the wistful little girl and the sad, too-mature face of her aunt.

Setting the frame on the dressing table, Cat said aloud, 'There you are, my flowers. Welcome to the good life.'

Refreshed by a quick shower, Cat wound a bathsheet around her and walked into the bedroom, almost colliding with Nick.

'Oh!' she exclaimed, scarlet to the tips of her ears.

He was clad in a cotton robe, imbuing that most prosaic of garments with sinful male glamour. His shoulders seemed much broader, his legs longer—and his eyes, she realised, were taking in her lack of clothes, the slim bare whiteness of her legs and shoulders.

'Sorry, I did knock,' he said curtly, and brushed past her into the bathroom he'd claimed for his own, closing the door behind him decisively.

Shaken, Cat shot into her dressing room, deciding to acquire a robe as soon as possible. Any sort, provided it covered her better than this bathsheet.

When he came back she was decently covered in a sleeveless blue dress that reached her ankles. The neckline scooped low enough to reveal the slight swell of her breasts, while the thin material swirled around her legs.

Lean and dark and dangerous in well-tailored black trousers topped by a tawny casual shirt several shades lighter than his eyes, Nick walked in without knocking, rolling sleeves back to show sinewy forearms.

'I'll put money into an account for you,' he said abruptly. 'You'd better buy whatever else you need.' He meant a dressing gown.

It took all of her composure to reply, 'Thank you.'

'It's inevitable that we'll meet in here occasionally.' He looked up, and something in his eyes sent shudders of response through her like tiny, persistent electric shocks.

Coolly, deliberately, he scanned her from the top of her chestnut head to her feet, almost bare in heeled blue sandals. 'Fortunately you're not a blushing *ingénue*.'

Her husband had never made her feel like this—as though some outside agency had sharpened her senses to an unbearable pitch. She could even smell Nick, she thought with alarm—a kind of tangy, male freshness, with an undernote of powerful sexuality that stirred her unbearably.

'Fortunately,' she agreed in her most neutral voice, wishing she could think of some snappy come-back.

'Do you ever wear anything other than blue?'

'What?' Startled, she said, 'Sometimes I wear tans and other colours that go with my hair.'

'But you concentrate on blue.'

What did he mean? Aloud she said, 'My father liked me in blue. I suppose I've got used to wearing it. It suits me.'

'It certainly does.' His eyes went to her hand. 'Put the ring on.'

'Of course. I'd forgotten...' Hating the beautiful thing, she took the ring from the dressing table and thrust it onto her finger, trying to hide her trembling hands.

Nick said, 'Oh, what the hell!' and came up to her in a silent, lethal rush.

Cat looked up sharply, her eyes enormous in her face.

'The whole idea of this charade,' he said between his teeth, 'is to convince Francesca that we're passionate lovers. If you flinch every time I come within six feet of you it's not going to work.' His eyes moved past her to the photograph on the bedside table.

He didn't have to threaten her; Cat knew exactly what he meant. No convincing, no money.

So when he tilted her face she didn't resist. But instead of the onslaught she expected, his kiss was light, the merest skimming of lips over her cheekbones—tantalising, gentle, almost reassuring.

After several seconds Cat's breath sighed out and she swayed towards him. He laughed, a simple indrawing of breath, and kissed his way to the lobe of one small ear.

She felt his arms slide around her. 'You have such soft skin,' he said deeply. 'Like pale silk, smooth and clear and flawless...'

Her heart began to hammer. How could he do this—set fire to her with a few light kisses? Oh, he knew how to play a woman! Mutely, without volition, she relaxed against his hard strength.

When he bit her earlobe she jumped. Instantly he lifted his head. 'Did I hurt you?' he demanded.

'N-no.' She shivered. 'It just felt... I've never... I wasn't expecting you to do that,' she finished lamely.

'Did you like it?'

Keeping her head down, she said in a choked voice, 'You know perfectly well how I feel.'

He silenced her by doing it again, and although she was expecting it, she still felt that tiny shock run through her system, prickling across her skin and melting her spine.

She waited breathlessly, but this time he kissed a certain spot beneath her ear; the hairs on the back of her neck lifted as a jolt of raw sexual energy tore through her.

And she suddenly hated those women who had given him such expertise.

'You're very good at this,' she said colourlessly.

He held her for a moment, and then let her go. 'You certainly know how to make a compliment sound like an insult,' he said, his eyes narrowed and cold.

Ashamed, she said, 'I didn't mean it as an insult.'

He shrugged. 'It doesn't matter. Yes, I've slept with more than one woman. Francesca is also experienced, and if we're going to convince her...'

He bent his head, taking her mouth without tenderness, without anything but a ruthless dominance, asking nothing but surrender.

Ashamed of her leaping, incandescent response, Cat jerked her head back, and when Nick refused to let her go she clenched her fist and punched him fiercely in the ribs.

She made as much impression as if she'd been pummelling concrete. He did release her, but only to study her indignant face with a chilling, dispassionate gaze.

'Yes, you look kissed,' he drawled. 'Not at all virginal.'

She said in a hard voice, 'I should hope not, because I'm not a virgin.'

One dark brow lifted. 'You could have fooled me,' he drawled, then looked at his watch. 'Time to go down. And remember, you're the hostess here.' He let the silence drag before adding, 'You do it so well; you're clearly a fast learner.'

Because Glen had been intolerant of mistakes. Cat opened her mouth to tell Nick exactly what she thought of him when there was a knock at the door. She froze.

Eyes on her face, Nick said quietly, 'Open it.'

It was Francesca, carrying what appeared to be a small case. Her gaze flew beyond Cat, yet she managed to incorporate both of them in her smile. 'Sorry to intrude,' she said pleasantly. 'Nick, would you put this in your safe? I know you have no crime here, but I'm too well trained to leave it in my room.'

'Certainly,' Nick said coolly. 'The safe's on the ground floor.'

Jewel case in hand, he left the two women at the bottom of the stairs. 'I'll be along in a minute,' he said.

'Sensible man,' Francesca murmured when he'd disappeared along the corridor. 'I'll bet no one knows where his safe is.' She gave Cat a lazy smile that didn't quite reach her eyes.

Time to play hostess. Cat said, 'We thought we'd have drinks out on the terrace. I love this time just before dusk, when everything is still and warm and waiting.' Her lips felt full and tender, and she was acutely aware that Francesca's glance had flicked across them.

'Well, it's warm for New Zealand,' Francesca said with another half-smile, walking beside her. 'Waiting for what?'

Feeling over-dramatic, Cat made sure her voice revealed no signs of defensiveness. 'For the night,' she said lightly.

Francesca laughed. 'Oh, you lovers,' she cooed. 'How long have you been together?'

Nick and Cat had discussed this. 'Some time,' she parried vaguely, 'but I only moved in here yesterday.'

From behind, Nick said, 'Cat stayed in Auckland to sit her finals.'

He was completely convincing, Cat thought; no lies, no hint of evasion. She realised anew how very good he must be in the cut-throat, buccaneering world he'd chosen. And the smile he gave her was a masterpiece. Not an open invitation to seduction—he was too subtle for that—it still promised all the delights of sexual experience.

'What are your plans?' Francesca asked edgily. 'Do you plan to work now you've got your degree?'

'Yes,' Cat said before Nick could answer. She opened the door into an informal living room and stood back to let the other woman go ahead.

Francesca sent a glance over her shoulder to Nick, her expression amused. 'Do I detect a certain amount of defiance there?'

'You do,' Nick returned smoothly, ushering Cat into the big room with its huge doors leading out onto yet another terrace, 'but we'll work it out.'

Francesca laughed at him. 'In other words you think you can get your own way.' Her gaze transferred to Cat's face. 'I don't know,' she said thoughtfully. 'She's got a very stubborn chin. I wonder if you've finally met your match, Nick?'

His broad shoulders lifted. 'I'm gallant in defeat,' he said with another intimate smile at Cat.

He was good, she thought angrily, and fluttered an upwards glance through her lashes in return, maliciously pleased by the sudden darkening of his eyes.

They walked through the informal living room and out onto another terrace. Mrs Hannay had laid a table with more candles, and with flowers, softly scented and palely glimmering in the late evening light.

'Gallant? That's not the buzz in business circles,'

Francesca said drily. 'When Dad talks about you he uses words like "initiative" and "courage" and "decisiveness" and "sheer, ruthless determination".' She sent him a slanted look. 'As well as "brilliance"—all the macho qualities. He probably thinks that gallantry is for losers.'

'There's a place for it,' Nick said calmly, walking across to a table that held a tray of drinks. 'Enemies are bad for business. What will you have, Francesca? Gin and tonic?'

'How sweet of you to remember, darling.'

Although Cat couldn't relax she found some pleasure in the beautiful surroundings. And, in spite of his demand that she use her skills as hostess, Nick directed the evening, laying down the boundaries of the conversation, deflecting with grace and good humour all Francesca's attempts to flirt with him, and he was always there for Cat, both a threat and a shield.

Francesca was an excellent guest—witty, entertaining, intelligent. Nevertheless, her green eyes were watchful and astute as they moved from Nick's angular face to Cat and back again.

Much later, taking off the Tanzanite ring to put it back into its box, Cat realised that her nerves were strung taut. When Nick knocked on the communicating door she flinched.

Get a grip, she ordered. But her hands shook as she snapped the little box shut and her voice sounded shaky and uncertain. 'Come in.'

Once inside he said, 'You did well.'

'Thank you. It wasn't difficult.'

'But now you know why this charade is necessary.'

She nodded and moved across the room, sitting on one of the chairs in the window. 'I thought you might be exaggerating, but my presence here is most definitely a disappointment to her.'

Nick said quietly, 'I like Stan, and I have to deal with him in business. I like Francesca too, and I don't want to embarrass or humiliate her. By the way, wear something sexy to bed tonight.'

'If you think—'

He broke into her heated words with the cutting precision of an ice axe. 'She's not going to give up so easily.'

Cat shook her head in astonishment. 'Surely she won't come knocking again?'

'She's her father's daughter,' he said abruptly. 'Persistent and stubborn.'

Frowning, Cat told him, 'There's just one minor point; I haven't got anything sexy. I wear T-shirts to bed.'

His black head inclined towards her dressing room door. 'Then it's as well I ordered a few suitable things the other day; when they arrived this afternoon Mrs Hannay put them away for you. Choose something that looks as though it's made to be taken off lovingly and slowly.'

Although his eyes were hooded and his voice remained level, almost impersonal, some inflection to the words—or perhaps the glinting light beneath his lashes—robbed her bones of stiffening. Dry-mouthed, she muttered, 'All right.'

'I have the utmost confidence in you.'

Hours later, clad in an exquisite drift of pale ivory silk, Cat tossed in bed and murdered sleep by wondering whether he'd ever been Francesca's lover.

But nothing could spoil the frightening, highly suspect pleasure she'd felt at his final words.

For a few seconds, she hoped, he might have forgotten that she'd been Glen's wife and seen her as a real human being.

Such sweetness was almost more dangerous than the heated passion they aroused in each other, yet she was smiling when she finally drifted into sleep.

*   *   *

She woke to a knock on the door, and the sudden dipping of the mattress on the other side of the bed.

'What?' she yawned, struggling to sit up.

From too close, Nick said quietly, 'It's all right.'

'Oh!' Forcing her lashes up, she swivelled her head to peer at him in the soft, pearly light of dawn.

He must have arrived only seconds before, but he looked as though he'd been in bed with her all night. While she peered incredulously at him he threw back the bedclothes and got out, leaving behind his scent and the indentation of his long body and his head.

Cat gulped. He wasn't wearing anything.

Pulses hammering, skin burning, she clamped her eyes shut and slumped back into the pillow, but as she listened to the whisper of fabric she couldn't banish the image of Nick, lean and golden and sleekly muscled, radiating a primal power that brought every cell in her body to instant, singing life.

'Coming,' he called calmly after another knock.

Following the soft click of the opening door, Cat strained to hear what Francesca was saying in a breathless voice pitched too high.

'Riding?' he said without expression. His voice became clearer, as if he'd turned. 'Darling, do you want to go riding?'

Dimly Cat remembered she had to convince the older woman that Nick wasn't available. Yawning again, she climbed out of bed and walked towards him, glad she'd chosen a flimsy nightgown that made the most of her small accomplishments; Nick snagged her as she came within reach and pulled her against his chest.

He smelt like sex—dangerous, darkly disturbing, an erotic experience in itself. 'It's the middle of the night,' she managed to say hoarsely.

Determinedly smiling, Francesca stood just outside the bedroom. 'Lazybones! Or perhaps you don't ride?'

'I can ride,' Cat said with precarious dignity. If she moved her cheek a bit she could feel the gentle rasp of Nick's chest hair on her skin, and it was incredibly sensuous to stand there enfolded by his body heat.

His arms tightened around her. 'Do you want to ride now?'

'I—well, yes, I suppose so.' Yes, she thought urgently—replace one sensuous experience for another, this time without the disturbing overtones of sexuality.

He said, 'We'll be down in ten minutes.'

'Great!' Francesca walked away, straight-backed, her shoulders held so stiffly she had to be uncomfortable.

Nick dropped his arms, giving Cat the opportunity to back a couple of steps from him. When he'd closed the door she said in a worried voice, 'It looks as though she's really in love with you.'

'She's not,' he said brusquely. 'Although she probably doesn't realise it, she's setting out to give her father what he wants—grandchildren.'

Nick's children. An odd heat gathered in the pit of Cat's stomach. She said, 'Are you sure?'

'He was teasing her about it the last time they were here.' Nick shrugged and went on, 'Before that she was flirtatious—she flirts as easily as she breathes—but there was nothing serious about it. Now she means business, but there's still nothing personal about it. Any reasonably presentable man who's won her father's respect would do. When I marry I plan to be more important in my wife's eyes than a stud, chosen to father children.'

A complicated mixture of sensations clutched Cat. She banished them—now was not the time to wonder whether he had a candidate in mind for this wife. Not altogether convinced at his reading of Francesca's intentions, she said with a wan smile, 'I hope she doesn't keep ambushing us.'

Nick looked down at her, his eyes half closed, his mouth a thin line. 'This had better be the last time,' he said grimly. 'I wonder why she's so suspicious.'

'Perhaps because she knows I haven't been here long.'

'Possibly.' He didn't seem convinced. 'Come on, get ready. Have you got clothes to ride in?'

'Jeans,' she said, adding, 'I didn't know you rode.'

He lifted one brow. 'During the school holidays Glen often sent me to his cousin's place, a sheep station outside Gisborne. Their kids taught me well enough so I can stay on most horses.'

CHAPTER SEVEN

THIS was an understatement. Following Nick's big roan gelding along a path between pine trees, Cat admired his complete ease and command, the stylish horseman's grace.

Francesca was even better. 'I grew up on a cattle station,' she told them when Cat complimented her. 'Been riding since long before I could walk.' She chirruped at her bay gelding as they came out onto a long paddock. 'Come on, lovely,' she crooned, and set it into a raking gallop, closely followed by the other two.

Ahead Cat saw a fence, separating this paddock from one that held cattle. She began to rein in her mannered mare well before, but the other woman kept going, her hair flying out under her helmet as she headed for the fence.

Nick called, 'No, Francesca!'

Such was the crack of authority in his voice that Cat wasn't surprised when the gelding slowed into a canter, and then to a walk.

'Spoilsport,' Francesca tossed over her shoulder.

'I don't want you jumping into the middle of the cattle,' he said, reining in beside her. 'They're my manager's pride and joy, and he'd probably resign if anything happened to one of them.'

With a shrug Francesca asked Cat, 'Is he always so masterful?'

'Always,' Cat returned solemnly.

Nick grinned. '"Masterful" is a word that's so out of date it's an insult.'

Francesca turned her horse with the other two and they

set off back towards the house. 'Perhaps you're a man from the past,' she said, still smiling with determination. 'The kind of ruthless, dominating, competent, authoritative man that women secretly long for even when they say they don't want them.' She gave a gurgle of laughter at Nick's sardonic expression. 'OK, I'll stop teasing. You know, this would be a fabulous place to bring up children.'

'New Zealanders like to think the whole country is a good place to bring up children,' Nick said smoothly.

He turned his head as though he felt Cat's eyes on him, and something passed between them—a shared emotion that for some strange reason thrilled her.

Be careful, she told herself. You're here to do a job. Yes, you find him incredibly exciting, and thanks to Francesca's prying the situation is about as provocative as it can be, but that's as far as it goes. He's dangerous.

She shivered and her hands tightened on the reins, summoning a reproachful toss of the head from her mare. Forcing her fingers to relax, she realised bleakly that she now wanted more from Nick than his simple, uncomplicated lust. Respect, she thought giddily. Yes, it had to be respect, and she had about as much chance of getting that as she did of achieving invisibility.

The sun beat down, hot and enervating, reflecting back from the placid waters of the pool so that although the two women lay under sun umbrellas their bodies were bathed in shimmering golden light.

'So when do you two get married?' Francesca lifted a languid hand to swat a marauding sandfly away from her long, bare leg.

Cat made a production of putting down her novel. 'We haven't discussed that yet,' she said truthfully.

The other woman turned her head to look at her. Cat was

wearing a gauzy shirt over her comparatively modest bathing suit, but Francesca's superbly cut two-piece made the most of her full breasts and elegant legs. 'Not discussed a date, or not discussed a marriage?' she asked bluntly.

Equally bluntly Cat returned, 'That's none of your business.'

Francesca's face froze. 'Who the hell do you think you are?'

'I know who I am,' Cat said equably. 'What I don't know is why you're so interested in my affairs.'

'Just this affair,' Francesca snapped. She started to say more, but voices inside the house silenced her.

When Nick emerged Cat was busy pretending to read and Francesca was lying on her stomach in the lounger, face turned towards Cat but her eyes obstinately closed, her graceful limbs and magnificent body displayed with panache. Why, Cat wondered, didn't Nick just marry her and let them all off the hook?

And was appalled at the wave of desolation the thought aroused.

He came over and sat on the side of her lounger, and bent his head to drop a quick, light kiss on her shoulder. 'How's it going?' he asked.

The touch of his mouth burned into her skin. Cat saw Francesca stiffen, then relax. Breathlessly, regretting the devil's bargain she'd made with Nick, Cat said, 'It's too hot to read. I should go for a swim.'

Her gaze lifted from the dancing, dazzling waters of the pool, traced Nick's profile as he said something to Francesca.

'That's a sombre look,' Francesca said. As Cat looked across in startled confusion, the other woman sat up. 'Sad thoughts, Cathy?'

'A difficult choice for tomorrow's menu,' Cat returned lightly.

'I've just remembered where I've heard of you before,' Francesca said, her voice almost a purr. 'You're Glen Withers's wife, aren't you?'

'Widow,' Nick told her in a flinty voice.

Francesca's mouth curved. 'And he was *your* mentor—dragged you out of the gutter and all that. How cosy,' she murmured.

Holding the other woman's eyes, Nick took Cat's hand. '"Cosy" seems an odd word to use,' he said in a pleasant tone that didn't hide the steel running through it.

Francesca gave him a level, what-have-I-got-to-lose? stare. 'If the cap fits... What would Glen think of his wife—widow—ensconced in your bedroom?'

'He'd hate it,' Nick said ruthlessly. 'However, it's been two years since he died; he wouldn't expect her to grieve for the rest of her life.'

'Did anyone ever find out,' Francesca asked softly, 'why he committed suicide?'

Cat gasped as Nick's fingers tightened unbearably around hers. Before he could speak she said fiercely, 'Glen didn't commit suicide! The idea's ridiculous. He was so full of life—he had plans for the next twenty years! His death was a horrible accident. He always drove too fast, and he was jet-lagged—he'd just flown straight back from England.'

Francesca drawled, 'So what caused the rumours?'

'There are always rumours when a high-profile person meets an untimely end,' Nick said, every word even and controlled. When Francesca lifted her brows in disbelief he went on in the same uncompromising tone, 'Cat was overseas for a year after Glen died, working in a clinic in Romit. Yes—' as the other woman's face altered '—during the civil insurgency. She didn't come back to New Zealand until the beginning of this year, and we started to see each other a few months after that.' He paused, then added on a silken, dangerous note, 'I'll have no hesitation in scotching any gossip that might come to my ears.'

Francesca held his gaze for a few further seconds, then seemed to crumple. 'Oh, forget it,' she said wearily. 'Sorry, I was prying, and that's not my usual style. But not even you can stop people talking.'

'I can,' Nick said lethally, his face carved into such an uncompromising hardness that Cat shivered.

Francesca lay back down and closed her eyes. 'I don't gossip,' she said indifferently.

Nick began to talk of an aircraft hijacking in Africa. Amazingly, Francesca followed his lead, displaying a shrewd understanding of the complex power-play of tribal and national rivalries that were involved, and ten minutes later it was as though that profoundly uncomfortable conversation had never taken place.

But it must have convinced Francesca that Cat and Nick were lovers. In the days that followed there were no more ambushes.

Yet when Cat conferred with the housekeeper over menus and organised trips and outings to keep the other woman entertained, when she presided at dinner parties and did her utmost to give Nick's guests a good time, Francesca's accusation about Glen played over and over in her mind. She tried to discuss it with Nick, but he refused.

'Leave it,' he said austerely. 'She was being unpleasant.'

But something wouldn't let her leave it, although the reason didn't reveal itself until she met Stan Barrington, who'd flown into Auckland the day his yacht arrived at the yacht basin. Nick drove them down to the huge, opulent vessel and they went aboard.

Tall and thin, with his daughter's green, intelligent eyes,

Stan shook hands as Francesca introduced him to Cat, finishing with, 'I'm really surprised you two haven't met before.' She gave her father a sunny smile and moved to link arms with him. 'Cat used to be Glen Withers's wife—the advertising man. The man who brought Nick up.'

'I remember him,' Stan said. 'I was sorry to hear of his death.'

And from some subtle note of sympathy in his tone she realised not only that he'd heard the rumours, but what had been niggling away in her mind these past days.

When Francesca had mentioned suicide Nick had been furious—but not surprised.

Cat couldn't say anything until she and Nick set off home after a dinner that made her realise the enormous difference between ordinary people and those like the Barringtons.

Because the races began the following day Francesca had wanted them to stay that night, but Nick had told her he had work to do. 'We'll be down mid-afternoon,' he'd said easily.

Francesca had pulled a face. 'I hope *you* didn't bring any work with you,' she'd said to her father.

He had shrugged. 'It's always there.'

Halfway home Nick commented, 'You're very quiet tonight.'

Cat said, 'Did I not pull my weight? Sorry.'

'I didn't mean that,' he returned shortly. 'What's on your mind?'

'You've known all along that some people thought Glen killed himself.' It wasn't a question.

The headlights from an oncoming vehicle flared across his face, revealing a grim, guarded expression. 'Yes,' he said.

Appalled, she whispered, 'What on earth gave them that idea?'

He glanced sideways at her. 'People like to gossip,' he said indifferently. 'Ignore it. And if anyone takes the same tack as Francesca did, ignore that too. Smile that sweet, bewildered smile at them and walk away.'

She said stubbornly, 'Had he said anything—done anything before he died...?'

'I don't know—had he?' Nick's voice was judicial, as though he was conducting an inquest.

'No,' she said quickly. But before he'd died Glen hadn't touched her for three months. She'd thought it was another affair.

'But?'

'But nothing,' she said firmly.

Nick said, 'Then there's nothing to worry about.'

'No. It's just that—Glen would hate to think people thought he was a coward.'

'Glen's dead,' Nick said brutally. And as she sucked in a breath he went on, 'He understood people, and you should know that the last thing he'd have cared about was gossip.'

Obscurely comforted, she said, 'You're right. He loved to shock people.' On impulse she finished, 'Thank you.'

Nick turned the wheel into the road that led to his house and wondered cynically whether she'd thank him if she knew just how much he'd kept hidden. Obviously she hadn't heard a word of the tornado of rumour and innuendo that had followed Glen's death when she'd been risking her life in Romit.

Whatever the reason she'd married Glen, she was serious about the child. Unless, of course, the child was only an excuse to get in touch again. Perhaps she wanted more money than Glen had left her, and who better to provide it than the idiot who'd admitted to a reckless passion for her?

His mouth compressed as he negotiated a pothole, the big car responding like a dream beneath his hands. Just like Cat, he thought with a hard, mirthless smile. She might be after security, but she came alive at his touch, her small body throbbing with the heat of her desire.

He'd spent the past few endless days getting her accustomed to the casual trail of his fingers across her cheek, to quick kisses dropped on the incredibly alluring nape of her neck, on the top of her head, on the satin curve of her seductive mouth.

Nothing heavy, nothing provocative, but each time he'd seen her breath come fast through her lips and that clear fugitive colour stain her silken skin.

Not long now, he told his eager body. Soon she'd come to him, driven by need, compelled by the same pitiless hunger that consumed him.

Tonight? He risked another glance at the pale oval of her face in the reflected glow of the headlights.

No. She'd been shocked by the knowledge that people had suspected Glen of suicide; she needed time to get over that. He banished the odd, inconvenient protectiveness that unmanned him now and then. She was lucky to be so tiny and fragile that she appealed to the basic male chivalry of his nature.

He'd waited six years for her; surely he had enough willpower to wait a few days more. When they made love he didn't want any memory of Glen overshadowing the moment. She'd be his entirely—Nick Harding's lover, not Glen Withers's widow.

Yawning, Cat turned over in the bed and forced her eyes open to watch the sun dapple the floor of the bedroom. She would, she thought as she reluctantly pushed back the covers, be sorry to leave Nick's house. And not just because from today they'd be on Francesca's turf. She grimaced. Make that deck.

No, she loved Nick's house—had felt completely at home from the moment she'd walked inside. The apartment she'd shared with Glen had been situated on Auckland's waterfront, not far from the yacht basin. It had been decorated in a chilly minimalist style that she'd tried to warm with flowers and indoor plants. Unfortunately the only flowers and plants that had looked good in the big, white rooms had been equally minimal and far from warm.

But Nick's home was light and airy, yet solid. In winter, when rain hugged the valley and the winds blew cold, it would be welcoming and warm and comfortable. A sly voice from the depths of her unconscious murmured that it would be perfect to bring children up in. Nick's children…

No yacht, however super, could live up to this.

'Are you all right? Aren't you feeling well?' Clad in his short robe, Nick padded through the door from the other room.

Startled, because they'd evolved a system of getting up that meant shuttling between dressing and bathrooms without meeting until both were fully clad, she kept her gaze fixed to his autocratic face. 'Have I slept in?'

'Only by a few minutes.' Like her, he wasn't letting his eyes wander, yet she fought a desire to slide back beneath the sheets. Fortunately her T-shirt covered her fully.

'Why did you cut your hair?' he asked without preamble. 'When we first met you wore it right down your back.'

Glen hadn't liked her long hair. 'Lovely, darling,' he'd said, 'but a bit milkmaidish for a grown woman.'

So she told Nick defensively, 'It made me look like a schoolgirl.'

'Why was that so bad? You were a schoolgirl.'

His cool response, charged with ironic undertones, flicked her nerves. 'Not quite,' she shot back.

'Was it Glen's idea or yours?' When Cat looked down at the sheet, he said, 'Glen's, then. I can understand why, I suppose, but it was a mistake. It doesn't make you look any more mature.'

'I like it. It's neat and easy to look after.'

He came across and sat on the side of the bed, smoothing a flyaway tress back from a suddenly hot cheek. His long fingers traced the curve of her ear, played with the lobe.

Cat's heart thudded so noisily she thought he must hear it, but if he did, his strong features remained disciplined, his mouth compressed; heavy lids half-covered his eyes.

'Would you grow it if I asked you to?' he asked softly.

Cat's pulses jumped. A quick, ferocious flare of sweet fire took her by surprise. 'It wouldn't grow much before Francesca and her father leave,' she said unevenly, aware that he was asking for much more than a change in hairstyle—and only too conscious of her overpowering desire to let common sense and prudence and self-preservation whistle down the wind so that she could give him what he wanted.

He bent his head and kissed—gently, lightly—the treacherous throb at the base of her throat. His mouth was a disturbing promise and a seductive threat.

Cat's breath caught behind the kiss; dizzy with need, she tried to pull away from this tender imprisonment but found she couldn't move.

'When I first met you,' he said in a raw voice that sent shivers scudding down her spine, 'I thought your hair looked like a cascade of fire. I couldn't believe it when you turned up at your wedding with it all shorn off.'

Dry-mouthed, desperate, she whispered, 'There was so much—it overpowered my face.'

'I didn't think so.' He eased himself down beside her and kissed the nape of her neck.

White-hot, delicious shivers pulled her skin tight; she'd never felt such pleasure before, so acute it came close to pain.

'Nick,' she muttered, trying to remember why this was a really bad idea.

'Cat—what you *do* to me…' His voice was almost drowsy, the words slow and slurred with desire.

His mouth was still a hair's breadth away and he didn't touch her, yet she couldn't pull back, held in thrall to his dark, enchanter's spell.

With one deliberate finger he stroked the length of her eyebrows. 'One sideways look from those smoky eyes sets me on fire.' He kissed her lashes closed, then that remorseless finger lightly followed the margins of her mouth. 'So ripe,' he murmured unhurriedly, 'promising forbidden delight and consuming pleasure.'

Lean, unhurried hands tilted her head. She forced up weighted eyelids to meet his gaze, golden and turbulent. Inside her something snapped, splintering into shards. Barely able to articulate the thought, she knew she'd never be the same again.

'Fiery Cat,' he said, kissing her between each word. 'Clever Cat, delicate and strong and graceful—I want you so much. Tell me you want me too.'

She couldn't deny him, yet something made her protest. 'Nick, this isn't—'

He crushed the rest of her answer on her lips, taking her mouth in a deep, hungry kiss. Conquered as much by his words as by his touch, she opened her mouth to the demand of his, yielding so completely that she never thought of resistance when he pressed her back against the pillows.

His smile revealed such fierce anticipation that she'd

have flinched if her own desire hadn't matched his with wild anticipation. Some hidden logical part of her brain warned her of danger, of never again being able to call her soul her own, yet her passionate need drowned any sensible promptings in a racing, glittering, violent surge of sensation.

Her arms slid beneath his robe, looping the wide shoulders, pulling him down. His skin burned against hers, heat enveloping her as they kissed and kissed again, each kiss leading her closer and closer to a fiery, elemental madness.

At last he lifted his head long enough to push the T-shirt up, over her face, off her arms. By then his own robe had been jettisoned and Cat was able to see the play of gleaming morning light across his shoulders and chest, the slow flexion of muscles beneath warning her of latent male power.

Caution was the furthest thing from her mind; magnificently reckless, she raised her eyes to his face as he surveyed her, her slight breasts tightening and colouring beneath the hot fire of his gaze.

'Beautiful,' he said, and kissed each peak, so sensitive to the touch of his mouth that she had to stifle a sharp moan.

He looked up swiftly. 'All right?'

She dragged breath into her lungs. 'Just…too much.'

'Yes,' he said as though it was a vow, and bent his black head again and took one nipple into his mouth.

Dimly Cat realised that her back had arched, that fire raced through her veins, that she was crumbling in an onslaught of sensation.

Too much—and yet she craved more.

When he lifted his head she had to stifle a disappointed cry, but his hand replaced his mouth, stroking her breasts as he kissed a circlet across her waist and explored the little hollow of her navel.

Feeling ran through her like arrows dipped in honey; sweet and pointed, each pulse hit a target in the pit of her stomach. That sensuous fire began to heat and twist until she was writhing with the intensity of it. She gripped his shoulders, found skin slick with sweat, and gripped harder, nails digging because she had to have something solid to hold onto or she'd go crazy, mindless with pleasure.

Nick found the demanding, sensitive centre between her legs, and she arched again like a bow and made a hungry little noise in the back of her throat.

'Yes,' he said again, sliding two fingers down and into her.

Pierced by joy, she said his name in a high, thin voice.

'Cat,' he said roughly, and bent his head and kissed the silken skin on her thighs.

'Please,' she whispered, pulling at him.

She felt the muscles beneath her hands go rigid; bewildered, she looked into his face, wilting at the ferocious control that masked his face, except for the betraying, brilliant gold of his eyes and his mouth with her kisses still marking it.

'Touch me,' he said.

Flushed, dry-mouthed, Cat ran her hands across his chest, exploring the small, hard points—strange male counterparts to her breasts—and the scrolled pattern of hair that arrowed down towards his waist and then onwards. Beneath her seeking hands he was heat and silk over iron—proud male, all virility.

When she touched the smooth, strong length of him he sucked in his breath and said on a strained note, 'No, not there. Not now. Not yet. You overwhelm me.'

For some reason this gave her a jolt of confidence. Shyly,

throbbing with the pleasure summoned by his experienced hands, she kissed his shoulder before some impulse drove her to bite into the hot skin, and then lick the place, filling her mouth with his taste—salty, tangy, an aphrodisiac in itself.

He said thickly, 'I have to get protection.'

'I'm taking the pill.'

'Nowadays that's not enough.'

When it was done he nuzzled the hollow of her throat, moved on to the outrageously sensitive spot beneath one ear that sent even more fiery messages through her overloaded body. And after that he kissed her.

Eagerly, passionately, she responded, and as their mouths clung he drove into her, taking her for all time.

Groaning, she arced up to meet his thrust, clung with her innermost muscles when he withdrew, and took him again as he returned. They set up a rhythm of advance and retreat, thrust and counter-thrust, linking and almost separating, then coming back together again.

Lost in a sensual daze, Cat concentrated fiercely on giving him everything she could, until to her astonishment the complex pleasure of joining began to alter; instead of lessening the keen edge of hunger it transmuted into a desperate, erotic compulsion, and her body was transfixed by sensations she'd never experienced before—an acute, avid need that tightened her muscles and stimulated her nerve-ends into unbearable activity.

Waves of sensation—at first tentative—swirled within her. Eyes fluttering shut, her tense body lifted to meet the hard strength of Nick's. Deep inside something built and built until she was submerged by the heat and power of him, the sensory overload of scent and touch and taste, of pressure and weight and sheer male energy.

Yet her own female power equalled it. Panting, she

strove to reach something, some pinnacle of experience like no other, crying out when a sudden, sharp ecstasy picked her up and threw her into another dimension, tumbling her through a vortex of shuddering, unknowable rapture.

And Nick went with her, arrived at that place as she did, cried out as she did, pumped into her as she welcomed him, and then, both of them tumbling like feathers in a summer breeze, he came down with her, until there was just the two of them in the big bed, reeling in the aftershocks of an intolerable delight.

Silently Nick turned on his side and pulled her towards him. 'Why are you crying?' he asked deeply.

Boneless with lassitude, so tired she could barely speak, she muttered, 'I don't know.' She blew her nose on the handkerchief he produced miraculously from somewhere, and wiped her eyes. To her dismay she felt a yawn begin. Clapping a hand over her mouth, she tried to stifle it without success.

Nick waited until the yawn had died and she'd abandoned the handkerchief, before saying, 'You're tired. Come here and sleep.'

'The Barringtons,' she said, resisting.

His eyes darkened and deliberately he turned her into his arms. 'We're not due at the yacht until after lunch,' he said. 'We've plenty of time.'

One hand pressed her head into his shoulder while the other lingered possessively on her hip. 'Go to sleep,' he ordered.

'But—'

He kissed her, sealing the words in. 'Sleep, Cat.'

Her eyes closed. Smiling, she turned her face into his chest and surrendered to exhaustion.

CHAPTER EIGHT

CAT woke alone in a bed that smelt of sex.

Chilled, she hauled the covers up to her chin and turned onto her back, bleakly surveying the ceiling. Nick had made love to her with an exquisite tenderness—as though she were a virgin, she thought, her forehead creasing.

Why had Nick been so gentle?

It was a stupid thing to worry about, and a swift glance at the clock told her she didn't have time to track the source of her concern. Moving stiffly, she got up and showered, refusing to allow herself to think, to remember, as she dried down before pulling on a pair of jeans and a thin cotton top in green and white stripes.

Combing her hair, she scrutinised the woman in the mirror. Her reflection looked back at her with the primeval knowledge of Eve in her eyes, secrets in the smile that curved her tender mouth.

'So that,' she whispered to that sexually aware woman who smiled at her, 'is what ecstasy is all about.'

Nothing would ever be the same again for her.

When Cat reached the bottom of the stairs, Mrs Hannay was coming along the hall. 'Morning,' she said, smiling.

Embarrassed, Cat returned the smile, but the housekeeper's eyes were guileless and open. 'Are you looking for Nick?' she asked. 'He said to tell you he's in the office.'

'Thanks.' Cat had never been inside the holy of holies, but this sounded more like a command than an invitation. She smiled again and turned, walking softly like a child summoned to the headmaster's office. Once outside the door she hesitated, then squared her shoulders and knocked.

'Come in.'

Fighting back a twist of apprehension in her stomach, she pushed the door open and walked in.

Nick wasn't sitting behind the huge desk, or the computer with its attendant machines. Instead he was standing in front of a picture—the portrait of her husband that had hung in the entrance hall of their apartment. Cat had given the portrait to Nick after her Glen's death.

Glen had admired the way the perceptive artist had caught his vivid, raffish charm, but he'd never noticed the underlying insecurity the artist had seen in his face.

Now Cat stopped just inside the door, reacting with age-old instincts to the danger in the atmosphere, so tangible she could smell it and taste it.

Without looking at her, Nick said conversationally, 'The rumours were right, you know—he did kill himself. He drove into that bridge quite deliberately.'

Whatever she had expected, it wasn't this. White-faced, she stared at him until she could find her voice. 'I don't believe you.' It sounded weak, each word stumbling after the other. Drawing painful air into her lungs, she forced a steady tone. 'Why would he do that?'

'He had cancer.' He put out a lean, beautiful hand, as though to touch the painted surface of the portrait, then let it fall to his side and turned to face her.

Golden eyes metallic, he continued, 'He thought he was bullet-proof, that nothing was ever going to kill him, so he wasted months before he finally went to a specialist. He was told that his only chance was an operation that would leave him both sterile and impotent.'

Cat shook her head, but those last three months of their marriage without sex suddenly made hideous sense.

'Yes,' Nick said, his voice cool and expressionless. 'Why didn't you make him go to the doctor, Cat? You must have known something was wrong when he didn't come near you.'

'I didn't know what—I thought he had a lover,' she said thinly, adding, 'It wouldn't have been the first time. Or even the second. And at the time I was so worried about my mother's health. Not that that's any excuse—I should have noticed that something was wrong with him.'

'He was facing the fact that if he had surgery and radiotherapy he'd be no sort of husband to you.'

'What?' Her voice cracked.

Still in that impersonal, chilling tone, he said, 'He never really understood that it wasn't sex you wanted from him, it was security. As long as he could provide you with that, you'd have stayed with him.' And after a tense moment he went on, 'That's why you married him, after all.'

A bitter, reluctant honesty forced her to acknowledge, 'I shouldn't have married him. You were right when you came to see me that day—before the wedding. I was looking for another father. But I did my best to be a good wife to him.'

Nick said, 'Before he went to England that last time he came to see me. He told me about his illness and said he'd decided that the only thing to do was make it as easy for you as he could.'

Tears stinging her eyes, Cat shook her head.

Mercilessly Nick went on, 'I thought I'd managed to convince him to fight it.' He smiled, a humourless movement of his mouth that froze her. 'I should have known better; once Glen made up his mind to do something, he always did it. He'd worked it all out very carefully so you'd be protected. He knew that everyone would blame jet lag.'

Convinced in spite of herself, she sank into the nearest

chair, her thoughts whirling in a hideous jumble. After a moment she said in a flat voice, 'I wouldn't have left him.'

'He felt that he was no use to you.' Nick's mouth twisted. 'So he killed himself, and I kissed you again after his funeral. I despise myself for that. The kiss I'd taken before your wedding had burned in my mind like a hot coal, tormenting me, never leaving me. When you touched me I—well, I lost control.'

'I was offering you comfort,' she said thinly.

She'd reached up and touched his cheek…and been enveloped in a firestorm of passion that for a few white-hot moments had driven everything but Nick from her mind.

'It might have begun like that, but you wanted me,' he said mercilessly.

She bit her lip. 'Yes.'

He gave her a dangerous, hooded glance. 'And I wanted you. Had you spent the four years of your marriage fantasising about me?'

Later his sneering question would hurt. 'No. I was so afraid of you I repressed everything, refused to think about it, refused to accept that I had—had wanted you. I hid from my—'

'Unfaithfulness,' he supplied laconically.

Her eyes flashed. 'You have very stringent standards—standards Glen certainly didn't live up to. There were at least two other women while we were married.'

'They meant nothing to him,' Nick said with abrasive cynicism. 'And, yes, I know that's the classic adulterer's excuse, but they didn't. Perhaps he thought you wouldn't care.'

'He used infidelity as a punishment. When I insisted on going to university he started an affair.' She shifted in the chair, then looked up.

'I know,' he said, the polished opacity of his gaze hiding

his thoughts. He paused, then added with deliberate, bitter sarcasm, 'It's a familiar story—an older man and his young wife, and the young betrayer.'

'Except,' Cat pointed out clearly, 'no one betrayed anyone else—unless we count Glen's couple of meaningless episodes.' She allowed her scorn to colour the last two words. 'I might have been too inexperienced—and too stupid—to realise what I was doing when I married him, but I stayed faithful to him, and you never touched me or showed any interest in me when I was his wife.'

'I wish I could appease *my* conscience so easily,' Nick said with an unyielding stubbornness that reminded her of rock-bound cliffs.

She demanded, 'Why did you tell me this now? After we've—we made love?' He said nothing, and she went on slowly, 'I see. You're making sure I don't get any ideas of permanence.'

Until that moment she hadn't realised how many hopes and dreams she'd been indulging in the secret corners of her heart—dreams of living with him, of overcoming his distrust, of making him see her as she was, not a greedy temptress but an ordinary woman.

His perception of her she could have fought, but she didn't have a hope of altering his remorse for what he saw as betrayal.

She got up and faced him, her head held high. 'Glen killed himself because he couldn't bear the thought of being less of a man. Well, let me tell you something, Nick; sex is not all that a man is measured by! Apparently it didn't worry him that I'd be left alone, still grieving for my mother and shocked by his death.'

'He knew I'd look after you,' Nick said between his teeth.

Anger stripped away her last shred of control. 'How?

Emotionally? Surely he didn't expect me to forget about my mother, forget about him, and meekly let you rule my life? He knew me better than that!'

Tossing words over her shoulder, she turned on her heel. 'How utterly chauvinistic and feudal of him—passing me over to you like a discarded parcel! If he really believed he could organise us both from beyond the grave, how well did he know us?'

She ran up the stairs and yanked the sheets violently from the bed. Eventually her hands stopped; she stared at the pillows, still marked with the indentation of his head, and painful tears clogged her eyes and her throat.

All right, she had dreamed. How ironic that even though Nick wanted her, her tentative hopes had smashed against his iron-bound honesty. The powerful, elemental attraction between them meant little compared to his loyalty to Glen.

If he loved her he might be able to forgive himself—and her. But he would never love her.

She took the sheets and pillows down into the laundry and risked Mrs Hannay's disapproval by putting them in the washer and switching on the machine. Then she tracked the housekeeper down and begged a cardboard carton from her.

Armed with this, she ran back upstairs and packed efficiently and rapidly.

When she'd removed every trace of her presence, she straightened and looked around. This was the end. Unless the fates were incredibly unfair, she'd never see this lovely room again, never return.

Somehow, some time during the past few days, she'd fallen over the invisible edge between attraction and love; there had been no moment when she could say it had happened, no explosion of understanding, but it had happened. And because it was hopeless, if she was ever to achieve any peace of mind she had to cut clean away from Nick and make sure they never met again.

He came in as she did up the catches; she'd packed clothes for the yacht in the smart luggage Nick had bought her, but everything else went into an elderly suitcase.

'Planning your escape?' he asked with raised eyebrows. A hard note threaded his tone. 'We made a bargain, remember. If you don't keep your side, I won't keep mine.'

'I don't intend to back out,' she returned shortly, 'but Francesca won't be coming back here, so neither am I.'

Neither her face nor the tone of her voice gave anything away, and she kept her eyes shaded by the thick lashes. She had turned away from him, but Nick sensed that every muscle in her slim, eager little body was poised and taut. The familiar urgent hunger consumed him, clouding his mind with fumes of desire. He could have her whenever he wanted her, he thought cynically, recalling her unfettered response with a clarity that made his inconvenient body tighten in anticipation.

God knows, she was any red-blooded man's dream of the perfect lover—hot as hell, sweet as heaven, passionate and willing and addictive.

And that was the problem, the emotional grenade that had been flung from the blindside to explode into his life. If he took her again, would he ever be able to give her up? Instead of sating himself in her, he might find himself unable to live without her.

Glen had killed himself for her. She certainly hadn't stayed faithful to his memory—unless she'd begun taking the contraceptive pill after she'd met Nick again.

Another, terrifying thought iced over his words. 'I don't expect you to,' he said evenly. 'I know how big you are on responsibility.'

She lifted her head in an abrupt movement. He saw quick

pain in her smoky eyes, and had to stop himself taking a step towards her.

For a forbidden moment he'd wondered what it would be like to see her pregnant with his child.

Francesca met them at the gangplank. Dressed in white linen, she matched the motor yacht, a mini-liner that by some miracle of the boat designer's art managed to appear graceful in spite of a helicopter pad and the pieces of navigational equipment that cluttered the short mast.

Eyeing her hostess, Cat wished she had legs that went on for ever and the inborn self-confidence that enabled her to ignore the interested stares of passers-by.

'Come aboard, come aboard,' Francesca urged, smiling at both of them although her eyes lingered compulsively on Nick.

In spite of a feverish flare of possessiveness, Cat didn't blame her. Compared to him, every other man in sight looked pale and ordinary and totally lacking in anything that might attract a woman. Oh, you've got it bad, she thought cynically as she walked up the narrow gangplank and onto a wide area at the stern of the boat.

'This is where we park the tender when we're sailing,' Francesca said, indicating a fair-sized launch moored beside. 'It's a useful sitting-out place when we have big parties. Tonight's not big—it's just a nice, casual evening to introduce some visitors to some locals.'

She led them into a sitting-out area shaded by the overhang of the deck above. The previous day Cat had noticed the white sofas decorated with vast numbers of cushions in various permutations of blue and white; now she saw that there was also a bar and that the floral arrangements had been changed.

'I love the buzz—this regatta is a great occasion!'

Francesca was saying, smiling at Nick as though she couldn't help herself. 'I'm really looking forward to to-morrow's race—those big sailing yachts are so graceful. Did you know that the owners—' she mentioned three names that Cat recognised from the newspapers '—have bet millions on the result?'

Nick's brows lifted a fraction.

Francesca gave him a provocative sideways glance. 'You don't approve?'

'I'm not a gambler,' he said mildly.

Francesca flung back her head and laughed. 'Oh, no? Who left a high-paying job to go adventuring in the wild, unknown world of the Internet? Of course you mastered it, but it was a huge gamble at the time. And now you're diversifying, like all sensible tycoons.'

Cat felt like a total outsider. This was Francesca's world. And Nick's, she reminded herself painfully.

And just then, just there, standing in the vivid sunlight watched by the people jamming the wharves in holiday mood, water dazzling her eyes and sending shifting lights across Nick's dark, gypsyish features, she realised how *much* she loved him—dangerously, desperately, irrevoca-bly, as though ancient gods had decreed her fate at birth.

After they'd made love she'd known that nothing would be the same again, but now, when she'd accepted that they had no future, she understood the full bitterness of the cup she'd chosen to drink. For her there would never be another man; Juana would be the only child she'd ever be respon-sible for.

Making love to Nick had fanned that aching, repressed hunger to an inferno, but the knowledge that she loved Nick—completely and utterly and without restraint—had fundamentally altered her.

'Are you all right?' Nick asked tersely, taking her arm

as Francesca went ahead through large glass doors into the saloon.

Had that sudden, shattering moment of comprehension shown in her face? Cat stiffened her shoulders. 'Fine,' she said, walking like an automaton. Once inside she turned her face away from his narrowed, watchful eyes and pretended to look around.

Since she and Nick had made love everything seemed dream-like, overlaid with significance, as though on waking that morning she'd stepped through a curtain into another dimension.

Heat curled through her, licking at her skin, warming deep inside. Hastily she pushed the memories away.

The doors closed, cutting off the cheerful babble outside; Cat took a deep, surreptitious breath of the cool air.

'I hope you're not one of those poor people who get sick before they've even left the dock. If you are, don't worry.' Francesca smiled at her. 'We have a positive pharmacy on board for anyone with a weak stomach.'

Cat's returned smile showed her teeth. 'I don't usually get seasick,' she said lightly, 'but of course if the boat travels badly it could happen.'

Nick said, 'Is your father on board, Francesca?'

Francesca said, 'He's talking to Tokyo in his office—no, here he is!'

Stan came through a door at the other end of the huge room. He was frowning, a frown that cleared when he saw Nick.

'Hello, Cathy, welcome aboard,' he said, nodding at her. 'Nick, come with me and see what you think of this. Old Leo Orlich is up to something, and I have a feeling I know what it is.'

Francesca gave both men another of her brilliant smiles.

'When business calls we women know our place in the scheme of things. Cathy, I'll show you your stateroom.'

But Nick said, 'I'll only be a short time,' his golden eyes somehow commanding as they swept Cat's face before he switched his attention to the sheaf of papers Stan Barrington thrust at him.

Silently Cat walked beside Francesca the whole length of the main saloon, furnished with honey-gold timber panelling and enough white leather sofas and chairs to seat thirty or forty people.

How the very rich live, Cat thought, using surface cynicism to mask the part of her that could only see into the grey dreariness of her future.

Such unbridled opulence felt alien, disturbing. She set her jaw and told herself sternly to look on it as a glimpse into a world she'd never see again after this masquerade was over.

She followed the other woman into a large cabin.

'Here you are,' Francesca said casually. 'If you need anything, tell the stewardess when she comes to unpack for you. We're having drinks in an hour's time, so you've got plenty of time to change.'

Cat watched the door close behind her. She was on Francesca's territory now, and instinct warned her that Francesca intended to take no prisoners. If Juana was to get her operation, Cat would have to act very convincingly as Nick's lover.

Panic sheened her skin with perspiration.

The stateroom could almost have been in a house—a very luxurious house, she thought, eyeing the carpet on the floor and the clever use of built-in wooden furniture. A huge bed decorated in blue and white linen took up a good part of the room, and a white leather sofa stretched along one side.

Behind a door a small, superbly furnished *en suite* bathroom glowed in a glory of creamy pink marble and gold and glass. When Cat finished exploring she showered, wrapping herself in a vast blue bath sheet to go into the stateroom.

A casual party, Francesca had said.

Cat quelled a flash of unease by reminding herself that she knew exactly what to wear to a smart barbecue; this couldn't be too different. She chose an unstructured shift of silk several shades lighter than her hair, sleeveless and low-necked, the soft material barely skimming the curves of her body to end at her knees. With it she wore copper sandals with heels high enough to give her some presence.

Then she called on skills she'd almost forgotten to paint cosmetics into a delicate enhancement that was a defiant, if fragile, armour.

When, made-up and determined, she came out of the tiny bathroom, she saw Nick pulling out a pair of trousers from the wardrobe next to the one in which her clothes had been stowed while she'd showered.

Her stomach dropped into freefall. 'What are you doing?' she demanded. The room shrank around her.

His brows shot up. 'I'm deciding what to wear.'

Even dressed in jeans and a T-shirt he managed to look piratical—dangerous and graceful, at once charismatic and untamed, his straight nose and those high cheekbones stamping him with an indefinable otherness. His dynamic male authority pierced her defences with insulting ease.

'But—' And she stopped, her eyes going with hunted directness to the big bed.

Nick saw betraying colour beat up into her skin. Anger gripped him. 'Surely you didn't expect to sleep by yourself?'

Her lashes quivered. 'I thought… Francesca…'

Curtly he said, 'We've established that we're lovers, Cat. She's not stupid enough to try and separate us.'

Her luscious mouth tightened. 'I'm not going to sleep with you tonight.'

'You can spend the night on the sofa if you like, but you and I are sharing this stateroom.'

Lifting her chin to stare directly at him, she repeated in a hard voice, 'I'm *not* sleeping with you.'

'If you mean you're not going to make love, say so.'

Anger lit her eyes with hot blue fire. 'Very well, then,' she snapped, 'I'm not going to make love with you.'

'Why not? You didn't mind this morning,' he said brutally, wanting to hurt her even though he'd come to exactly the same decision. Despising himself for his lack of control, and even more at the shame that whitened her skin, he finished, 'And if you ask for another cabin this whole charade will have been wasted.'

Her white teeth met with an audible snap. 'Of course I won't ask for another cabin.'

Still tense with repressed passion, he nodded. 'I'll sleep on the sofa.' And, crass as a high school boy on his first date, he said, 'You look—lovely. I like that colour on you.'

The stiff words hung between them. A frisson of need shivered through Cat. Awkwardly, swiftly—anything to break this sensuous enchantment!—she muttered, 'Thank you.'

As though he regretted the compliment he said abruptly, 'I'll shower and get changed.'

Bonelessly she lowered herself into a chair and closed her eyes. A passing vessel made enough wake to set the boat gently swaying. Trying to relax her rigid shoulders, she leaned back in the chair, listening dreamily to the faint hiss of water in the bathroom, and then the hum of an electric razor.

This morning his beard had been like rough silk against her skin; she could still feel that sensuous friction on some deep cellular level.

She wriggled, trying to repress the sudden heat in her body as Nick came silently back into the stateroom, a towel hitched around his lean hips.

Cat picked up a magazine and pretended to read it as he dressed, acutely aware of the flakes of colour burning the skin over her cheekbones. At least the cosmetics would subdue the worst of it, she thought, keeping her gaze pinned unseeingly to the page as Nick moved around the cabin.

In a surprisingly short time he said sardonically, 'You can look now.'

Black hair gleaming, his autocratic face newly shaven, the sight of him hit Cat like a blow. At least those tanned shoulders and chest were now covered by a fine cotton shirt, and trousers—fitting so well that they must have been tailored for him—hid his narrow hips and long legs.

Cat gave him a cool smile.

'Still sulking?' he asked dangerously. He came across the carpet in two quick strides and pulled her from the chair, lifting her face with a merciless hand so that she was forced to meet that cold, predator's gaze.

'No.' Defiantly she pressed her lips together.

His fingertips slid between her lips. Sensation—violent, powerful, achingly sweet—roared through her, locking out common sense and logic.

Above the sound of her heart thudding in her ears, Nick asked quietly, 'So tell me why you made love to me this morning as though you've been starving for me as long as I have for you.'

'No,' she breathed, witless with longing.

The finger between her lips moved to the corner of her mouth, then traced the outline. So gentle, she thought dazedly, yet so potent. Could he feel the shallow flutter of her breath on his skin, the rapid thunder of her pulse? Yes, he knew what his closeness did to her.

His mouth quirked. 'No, you can't tell me, or no, you don't want to?'

'Both,' she whispered, and pulled against his grip.

Dropping that tormenting, inquisitorial hand, he let her go, but she saw the smile that curved his mouth. If he wanted to make love tonight, could she resist?

Worse, would she want to?

'Wear these,' he said, taking a jewel case from a drawer and holding it out. When she made no attempt to take it he said sardonically, 'They won't explode. Think of them as stage jewellery.'

They were pearls, a string of lustrous blue-black spheres.

'Something else from Morna?' she asked in a high voice.

'Yes.' When she shook her head he said, 'Don't be foolish, Cat,' and looped the warm chain around her throat. Determined hands on her shoulders turned her slightly so that she could see herself in the mirror that ran down one wall.

He said, 'They suit you.'

Cat's breath stopped in her lungs. She wasn't looking at the pearls; her eyes were locked onto the two of them together, her small slenderness overshadowed by his height, her hair like a flame against his shirt, broad shoulders offering protection and strength, her curves a potent contrast to his lean lines.

'Yes,' he said in answer to her unspoken response. He slid his arms around her and cupped her breasts in tanned, possessive hands, watching with heavy-lidded insolence as the sensitive nubs peaked.

'You can't deny this,' he said harshly. 'You've haunted my life ever since I saw you.' A shaft of mockery bright-ened his eyes. 'I thought that making love to you might kill it, because nothing could be as erotic as my dreams.'

Half hypnotised by his touch, she said, 'And is it dead now?'

'No. I was wrong. You're a hell of a lot more erotic than my most erotic dreams.' His hands moved slowly from her breasts to her waist, circling it. 'It didn't die for you either.'

Ripples of sensation surged from those experienced fingers, arrowing to her breasts, to the vulnerable junction between her legs. 'No, damn you,' she whispered defiantly.

He laughed deeply, his hands finding her hips and turning her against his aroused body. It was like walking into fire, into storm; she shuddered at the wildness engulfing her.

He was going to kiss her; she was already on tiptoe to meet his mouth when she heard voices outside, and said unsteadily, 'We have to go.'

'Yes,' he said, golden eyes hotly territorial. He waited until she blundered towards the door before saying, 'Put the ring on. I want everyone to know you're mine tonight.'

CHAPTER NINE

FOR the next hour, as she drank mineral water and ate a couple of small, tempting delicacies while chatting to the Barringtons's guests, Nick's last command lingered in Cat's mind. Although it had been tinged with a certain ironic detachment, he knew he had only to touch her and she was his.

She heard her name and turned, breaking into an astonished smile when she saw who stood there. 'Stephanie! When did you get back?'

'Three days ago.' After a quick hug Stephanie stepped back and surveyed her with narrowed eyes. 'I rang your flat but they told me you'd left, and so had the only other person who knew where you were. Of course they didn't know her address either. I was beginning to wonder whether I should start worrying. What one earth are you up to?'

Stephanie Cowdray and her gorgeous husband Adam were the only two people Cat had established a true friendship with during her marriage to Glen. Tall, red-headed, with an exquisite English skin, Stephanie had tried to persuade Cat to live in their house while she and Adam spent the past six months in England with her family, but the property where Adam bred his world-famous roses was too far out of town to be practical.

'I didn't let you know because I left in such a hurry,' Cat said now, 'but—'

'Tell her the truth,' Nick drawled from behind. 'She got carried off.'

Stephanie's blue gaze went from Cat's face to Nick's. She said, 'By you?'

'By me,' he said.

He wasn't touching Cat, but she felt him there. Her skin prickled in involuntary homage to his vital masculinity.

Stephanie said, 'I see.' It was impossible to tell what she was thinking.

Francesca said Nick's name. He frowned, but turned politely. 'Darling,' she said, 'there's someone I'd like you to meet.' She looked past Nick to Cat and smiled. 'Sorry to interrupt, but Mr Penn is the dearest man, and he does something so important for the American government that financial markets tremble when he frowns. I'll return Nick to you in good order, I promise.'

Nick nodded. 'I'll be there in a moment,' he said courteously, and smiled at Stephanie. 'We've met before,' he said. 'I'm Nick Harding. Your husband and I play squash together occasionally.'

Stephanie held out her hand. 'I hadn't forgotten you,' she said drily as they shook hands. 'How are you?'

'Very well, thank you. Is Adam here?'

Stephanie laughed. 'He's out on the aft deck swapping rose-growing tips with Mr Penn.'

'Roses?' Francesca demanded.

Stephanie gave her a dazzling smile. 'My husband breeds roses,' she told her lightly.

'He's well on the way to being the most famous rose-breeder in the world,' Nick told his hostess. 'His *Stephanie* has been top rose wherever it's been grown.' His smile was a masterpiece—appreciation for a beautiful woman without the faintest hint of sexuality.

'Oh, Adam Cowdray, of course!' Francesca said, her hostess's instincts reappearing. 'You'll be thinking I'm a total airhead! I'll just take Nick out to join the rose-fanciers, and then I'll be back and we can catch up.'

Nick's glance lingered on Cat's face. 'I won't be long,' he said, and in the deep voice there was both a promise and a warning.

Only then did he turn away to join his hostess.

Thoughtfully Stephanie watched them cross the crowded saloon. 'I wouldn't have thought that the Barringtons and Nick Harding had much in common.'

'Money, I suppose.'

'Cynicism doesn't suit you.'

Too late, Cat remembered that Stephanie's brother was a British tycoon who'd forged another enormous fortune to go with the one he'd inherited. 'I'm sorry. That *was* cynical—and unkind.'

'Well, they are both on the southern hemisphere rich list,' Stephanie said fairly. 'And Nick's going to make the international list soon. No doubt Mr Barrington thinks a lot of him. Everyone does. Most people don't understand the Internet, but they do know that Nick practically controls it in this part of the world. Going out on his own was the best thing he's ever done. He was a brilliant adman, but he was wasted there.'

Cat smiled without humour. 'Glen believed that Nick was his creation.'

'He gave him his first chance,' Stephanie said judicially, 'but Nick would have got there on his own. He has that particular mixture of ruthlessness and intelligence and hard common sense that breeds tycoons.'

'You should know,' Cat returned with an attempt at lightness. 'That's a pretty good description of both your husband and your brother. Men like that are dangerous.'

'And intriguing.'

How to answer this? 'Intriguing' seemed a feeble word—

barely a step up from interesting!—and her emotions for Nick were far from feeble. Cat's shoulders lifted in a slight shrug. 'Oh, yes, definitely intriguing.'

'I thought you didn't like him much,' Stephanie said.

Cat hesitated. 'It's a long story.'

'And you're not sure you want to talk about it?' Stephanie said shrewdly.

'Well, not here, anyway.'

After a shrewd glance Stephanie said, 'I know your mother was eager for you to marry Glen; she told me once that her worst nightmare was dying and leaving you alone. I could see her point, although you're stronger than she ever gave you credit for. You can certainly look after your-self now—and you don't need any man, not even Nick Harding, as a prop. You might want him—'

Cat's face flamed. 'Is it so obvious?'

'I could have cut the tension with a knife! Just be careful, all right?'

'As careful as I can be when confronted by a force of nature.' She added with bleak pragmatism, 'I'm safe enough. Nick wants me, but he's determined not to do any more than that.'

'Even the toughest man,' Stephanie told her with amuse-ment, 'finds it hard to cope with that intense sexual pull. In fact, I think it's harder for the tough ones—they hate losing control. Nick might decide to do nothing about it, but he won't be able to kill it. You have to decide how you're going to deal with it.'

Automatically Cat said, 'Don't worry about me.'

'If you ever want a sympathetic ear, I'm here.' As though summoned by an invisible force, Stephanie turned her head, her face lighting up when she saw her husband.

Cat bit back a sigh. Adam Cowdray's intimidating face revealed nothing of his thoughts, but the smile he gave his wife hinted at his emotions, deep and solid and primal, pointing up only too clearly the hollowness of Cat's relationship with Nick.

An hour later, after a trip to the bathroom, she stood just inside the saloon door and looked around. The life she'd led with Glen had been comfortable, secured from any shadow of poverty, but this was something else again. Amongst the crowd in the saloon were faces she'd only ever seen on the international news.

And this was Nick's world.

Watching him, tall and dark amongst some of the most powerful men on earth, she thought that he radiated authority and dynamic energy. He might have grown up on the backstreets of Auckland, in a family that could give the word 'dysfunctional' a whole new meaning, but his integrity and brilliance and that cold, sure intelligence had earned the respect of the men he was talking to. In every way that counted, he was their equal.

Yet their opinion didn't matter, she thought with a flash of insight. Nick had his own standards, his own values, his own ambitions; he didn't care what others thought of him.

As though he sensed her watching eyes, he looked across the intervening heads and smiled, a swift, sexy movement of his lips that melted her bones. His head moved in a silent command.

Pride urged her to turn on her heel, until she remembered why she was there and made her way across to him.

'Hello, darling.' He slid an arm around her, holding her loosely against him with unnerving possessiveness as he introduced her.

One of the men, short and a little over-dressed in an elegant dinner jacket, fixed pale eyes on her and asked in a strong English accent, 'You're a New Zealander, I assume, Ms Courtald?'

'Yes.'

Julian Forrester looked up at Nick. 'You breed them pretty here.'

'Clever too,' Nick said, something in his even tone stirring the hair on the back of Cat's neck.

She moved uneasily, aware of his arm tightening around her, aware too of the boldness of the other man's eyes.

Adam had been watching. 'Don't take her lightly,' he advised the other two men. 'She'll call you on anything stupid you might find yourself saying.'

'I wouldn't be so rude,' she said, laughing a little at him. 'I only do that to friends.'

'You must have an exciting life, Harding.' Julian Forrester's observation hung on the air.

'As much excitement as I can cope with,' Nick agreed coolly, and before anyone could make any other comments he steered the conversation into other channels.

As Cat listened, she thought that she disliked the Englishman with the bold eyes. Adam was always good value, but the other man, a pleasant German, wasn't much interested in anything but the financial markets. She was glad when Nick called a polite halt and moved away.

'You've been drinking water since we got here,' he said. 'Would you like some champagne?'

'I think perhaps I would.'

As if summoned by magic, a waiter offered a tray. With an odd hitch to her breath, Cat smiled her thanks as Nick took two glasses.

'Shall we go outside?' he suggested, handing her one. 'It's quieter out there.' He smiled down at her. 'We can watch the night life.'

Heart skipping, she went with him sedately through the crowd and out onto the aft deck, which was indeed very quiet because it was empty.

'Oh, this is lovely.' Cat relaxed into one of the over-stuffed sofas and looked along the quay at the bustling restaurants and bars, heard the hum of a city enjoying itself. She wished that she and Nick had just met, without any baggage from the past, that they knew nothing about each other.

Except, common sense pointed out, in the normal course of events you'd have never met Nick. Glen had brought them together.

She stiffened as she felt the cushions of the sofa give. 'What are you thinking of?' Nick asked, settling back, long legs stretched out in front, a lean, skilful hand cradling his champagne flute.

For an even madder moment she was tempted to tell him, but she said instead, 'You bought the right necklace. Black pearls seem to be the rage this year. I've had three women ask me where they came from, and I've seen another two with stunning ropes. I gave everyone Morna's name.'

'Good. She could do with a little international publicity.'

Light glinted off the Tanzanite ring. Cat's hand stole up to the pearls, warm and smooth against her skin. She'd thought they'd be overdoing it, but some of the women in there wore jewels that looked very serious indeed. 'She's very talented,' she said.

'Very,' he returned without inflection. 'What else are they buying—apart from New Zealand wines, if my palate can be trusted?' He took a mouthful of the champagne. 'Although this is a good French vintage.'

'Crates of wine,' Cat agreed, 'especially white, although they were bandying about the names of some excellent reds. And garden furniture.' She settled back into the sofa.

His brows shot up. 'Garden furniture?'

Cat gave a sudden grin. 'One woman liked a brand of

chairs and loungers so much she bought out a warehouse-full of it.'

He laughed quietly. 'Then here's to the garden furniture makers and conspicuous consumption.' He raised his glass; after a moment's hesitation Cat followed, and together they drank a silent toast.

The tide had gone down while they'd been inside and the aft deck was now beneath the level of the quay, the overhang of the deck above shielding them from any nearby pedestrians. Inside the saloon, party-goers talked and laughed and manoeuvred, their noisy hum muted by the heavy glass doors. The scents of the sea and those from the great vases of flowers mingled with traces of expensive, sultry perfumes.

Cat sneaked a sideways glance. Nick's profile was sil-houetted against the light from within—harsh, faintly for-eign, beautiful.

Her heart opened to him, unprotected, defenceless.

Soon this interlude would be over. Nick would have put an end to Francesca's pursuit without hurting her too much, and Cat would have the money to pay for Juana's operation.

But how could she bear to live without Nick?

That stark question echoed despairingly through her as she sat with him, talking of nothing much and slowly sip-ping champagne in the friendly darkness, until Francesca came looking for them.

When most of the guests had left, including the Cowdrays, dinner was served in another room with those who remained—one of whom, Cat realised with a prick of unease, was the Englishman with the bold eyes.

After dinner Francesca said brightly, 'It's too early to go to bed. I believe there's quite a good nightclub along the wharf. Any takers? Cathy? Nick?' She glanced around with something like a challenge in her expression.

Nick said, 'Count me out, Francesca.'

Into Cat's mind sprang an image of that huge bed, but she'd made a bargain and she intended to stick to it. 'And me too,' she said.

With smooth urbanity Nick deflected Francesca's protests, but when Julian Forrester said, 'Don't blame you at all,' and smiled significantly at Cat, something hot and feral flashed in Nick's eyes. Only for a moment, and his face still remained unreadable, the strong features chiselled in lines of near-boredom, but it was enough to silence the other man.

'Oh, all right,' Francesca said, her ungracious words tempered by the smile she bestowed on everyone. 'Those of you who want to dance, come with me.'

There was a chorus of takers; as everyone else chattered down the gangplank and along the quayside, Stan said, 'How about a nightcap, you two?'

Nick took Cat's hand. 'Sounds a good idea.'

She could feel emotions running through his lean fingers—fierce, purposeful, a sizzling current both thrilling and disturbing.

In an intimate corner of the saloon Stan poured whisky for himself and Nick, and mineral water for Cat. Nursing the glass gave her an excuse to pull her hand away from Nick's.

'So when are you going to make an honest man of this young pirate?' Stan asked her, shrewd eyes going from one to the other as he sat down.

What the devil was this about? Nick thought savagely, poised to intervene. If Francesca thought she could use Stan to interfere, she'd soon learn her mistake. And so would Stan.

But Cat forestalled him. She said pertly, 'When I'm ready.'

Clever Cat.

Their host laughed and shook his head. 'I don't know about your generation. What's stopping you?'

Before Nick could say anything Cat looked directly at Stan, her lovely face serious. 'I married very young, before I really knew what I was doing.' Her voice dropped. 'This time I have to be certain I know what I'm doing.'

Nick had to admire her. She did it brilliantly, her face tilted slightly, her expression grave and almost wistful.

'But you've made up your mind,' Stan said thoughtfully.

Nick measured glances with their host. 'I've made up *my* mind, but I'm not going to let you bully Cat into something she isn't ready for.' He reached for her hand again, his body tightening helplessly as the slender fingers slowly gripped his. 'You'll be among the first to know when we've come to a decision,' he said, his lack of control over this unruly desire reinforcing his decision not to give in to it.

Stan gave a sharp nod. 'Fair enough,' he said, and changed the subject.

Half an hour later they made their various ways to bed. Once inside the stateroom, with the door closed behind them, Nick said harshly, 'I'll make sure that you're never left alone with Julian Forrester. One more crack from him and I'll push his teeth down his throat.'

Cat shrugged. 'Some men see all women as prey.' And because she had to put some distance between them, she added coldly, 'Or merchandise.' The Tanzanite ring flashed in the lights as she took off Morna's pearls.

'And what the hell do you mean by that?'

Weighing the blue-black spheres in her hand, she answered steadily, 'I'm not your fiancée, and after your refusal to go dancing there's no doubt that you wield the whip. I suppose you can't blame Forrester for thinking I can be bought.'

He towered over her, his tall, lean grace sending shivers the length of her spine. 'Neither an engagement nor a wedding ring separates women who can be bought from those who can't. Don't ever say that again,' he said with a lethal distinctness that made every word silkily menacing.

'Why not? It's what you think.'

There was an odd moment of silence. Nick's face was etched in lines of ferocious self-control, as though the emotions he leashed were so violent he didn't dare let them loose.

When he spoke his voice was soft, terrifying. 'I did at first. It wasn't until I met your mother and heard something about your upbringing that I understood your situation.'

'That's very big of you,' she said, hiding her bitterness with cold composure. 'You must have had some interesting conversations with my mother.'

'Enough to understand that you were a cherished child brought up to believe that men took care of women.'

She said evenly, painfully, 'That was part of it. But when I agreed to marry Glen I did honestly think I loved him.' After a long pause she added, 'Then I met you and you looked at me as though I were a slut.'

For a heart-stopping second he stared at her, golden eyes polished and shimmering, before turning away. 'I never thought that. You were very young. I didn't blame you for looking for an easy way out.'

Had he changed his mind about her? Quick hope surged inside her, a hope she didn't dare face. She thought he was going to say more, but he remained silent, his face closed against her, the hard-edged, gypsyish features unyielding.

Feeling as though she'd battered her head against a stone wall, she asked, 'Why was Stan prying?'

'He wants to be able to tell Francesca that she has no chance at all.'

'Oh.' Guilt crawled over her.

'Do you want the shower? I'll sleep on the sofa.'

Until then Cat hadn't realised that she had spent the whole day waiting for him to woo her into his arms, reverse her rejection of him with honeyed, sensual expertise.

Sick at heart, she blurted, 'Don't be silly.' She looked at the bed, all king-sized width of it, and added with a pale smile, 'There's plenty of room for us both to sleep in that without touching, let alone colliding.'

'Are you sure?'

'Yes,' she said, 'I'm sure. I'll have a shower now.'

When Cat came out the stateroom was empty. Silently she got into one of her new nightgowns and climbed into the bed, presenting her back to the other side as she courted sleep with determination. Half an hour or so later the door into the stateroom opened. Cat didn't have to sneak a look through her lashes; a sixth sense beyond sight and hearing recognised him immediately.

Cat clamped her eyes shut. After a few seconds she heard the door into the bathroom close.

Relax! she ordered her wilful brain, but it stayed mutinously alert until he padded back in. Still with her back to the other side of the bed, she forced air in and out of her lungs as he slid between the sheets.

This is what you want, she told herself sternly. No sex—no tender, tempestuous lovemaking to break your heart.

So why was she feeling so bleak and bereft?

'Go to sleep, Cat,' he growled.

Eventually she woke to dawn glimmering through the portholes; she stared at the ceiling with a puzzled frown that turned rapidly to recognition.

In spite of the air-conditioning, she'd kicked the bedclothes off. Shivering in the early-morning chill, she

slowly, carefully, turned her head. Nick was lying turned
away from her. Transfixed by the magical way a wash of
sunlight burnished the curve of his shoulder, how his hair
curled across the back of his neck, the sensuous contrast of
burnished skin and black hair against white sheets, she stiffened when she noticed faint scratches on his back.

Colour scorched along her cheekbones. Her fingernails
had marked him when she'd cried out his name and con-
vulsed beneath him in ecstasy.

This time yesterday, she thought, I hadn't made love with
Nick. I hadn't lived.

This time yesterday I didn't know I loved him. I knew I
was in danger, but I didn't understand that I was heading
for a broken heart.

This time yesterday she'd been almost safe.

Now, lying close enough to touch him, she understood
that in his arms she'd found out what it meant to be a
woman. Until Nick had made love to her with such heart-
shaking passion, she hadn't known that all happiness could
be bound up in one man.

The knowledge scored her heart and mind. Desperate to
avoid the pain, she tried to convince herself that she felt
better because he no longer despised her quite so much as
he used to.

The thought didn't comfort her at all. She wanted infinitely more than his grudging passion; she wanted the ecstatic highs as well as the inevitable lows, she wanted to
eat breakfast with him every morning, and have his children, and make sure he had eight helpings of fruit and
vegetables every day, and wonder why his socks ate each
other in the drawer.

She wanted to laugh with him and talk with him and
quarrel with him and make up with him; she wanted to lean
on his strength, to lend him hers. She wanted what

Stephanie had with her Adam—total trust, the confidence of a love grounded on rock.

She wanted everything, and it was all wrapped up in the love of the man who slept beside her—and that, she accepted bitterly, was cruelly unattainable.

Nick would never allow himself to love her; whatever feelings he had for her were an inconvenience to him.

He woke instantly, all senses alert, and rolled onto his back, his head whipping around. Dark gold eyes fixed on hers. 'Good morning,' he said, his voice sensually roughened by sleep.

'Good morning,' she replied with an odd formality.

Yawning, he stretched with the ease and complete unselfconsciousness of a great cat before turning towards her.

Cat's body sprang to urgent life. She had to clench every muscle to stop herself from touching that tanned skin, running her fingers across the beard-shadowed jaw and down over his chest...

Offering herself! she thought with disgust.

'You're so valiant and stroppy I forget how little and delicate you are,' he murmured, his gaze caressing her bare shoulders.

'Small and stroppy outwits large and lumbering any time,' she said, and laughed at his startled expression.

'Large and lumbering?' he drawled. 'Do I lumber?'

'No,' she said unevenly. 'You move like a panther, all grace and strength.'

For a taut, tempting moment their gazes locked. With a predatory smile he reached for her, his long fingers resting against the sudden thunder of her pulse at the base of her throat.

The gathering daylight picked out the autocratic framework of his face, emphasising the blade of his nose, the chiselled mouth and determined jaw. Cat's lashes drooped when she saw the telltale flush of arousal stain his flaring cheekbones.

'Panther? We're well matched, then, because at certain times you produce a feline smile that drives me crazy,' he said, his voice low and thick.

He lowered his head, and brushed his mouth across hers, taunting, tantalising her with an almost-kiss.

Cat's whole being rose in clamorous insistence, but although her eyelids closed on a moment of pure, agonising need she retained enough control to leash that overwhelming hunger, to stop her lips from clinging to his, to freeze and pull back, knotting her fingers in front of her.

He said something so explicit she flinched. She watched his hands clamp into white-knuckled fists. Without speaking, a muscle throbbing in his jaw, he swung out of the bed in one lithe movement.

Consumed by the brief touch of his mouth, her brain spinning into sensuous overdrive, she followed him with hungry, heavy-lidded eyes as he strode into the bathroom. Tall, naked and glowing bronze in the morning light, he looked like some primitive god from the beginning of time.

She was still lying in the bed when he returned, towel knotted around his hips, his shoulders and hair diamonded with a few last drops of water.

'Get up,' he said curtly as he walked across to the wardrobe.

It felt like a slap in the face. Driven by a sharp inner demon, Cat pushed back the bedclothes and stretched sinuously, fiercely glad that she was wearing one of the nightgowns he'd chosen, its ivory silk the exact colour of her skin.

She certainly had his attention now; his face hardened. 'It's not going to work, Cat—you were right, sleeping together is a fool's game,' he said coolly, aloofly, his voice so detached it sounded indifferent.

Yet anger raked the steady words like a jagged reef just below the surface of a smooth sea.

Prickled by humiliation, she got to her feet. 'How long are we on this yacht?'

'Today and tomorrow.'

She smiled obliquely. 'It's going to be interesting.'

His eyes glinted. 'To use your own words, exasperating rather than interesting.' But he couldn't hide the almost imperceptible alteration to his voice, his face, that signalled his response to her. 'Today we're sailing up to Kawau Island. Do you need seasick pills?'

'No, thank you, I have a cast-iron stomach.' And it was utterly stupid to feel her heart contract at this tiny evidence of consideration. It was no more than one would ask a stranger! 'I'm looking forward to it very much,' she flung over her shoulder on her way to the bathroom.

CHAPTER TEN

LUNCH was served on a small uninhabited island—a picnic set up by stewards and presided over by a chef. After that there was some jostling for position amongst the spectator fleet before the race began.

'It's a perfect afternoon,' Francesca enthused, sparkling like the day itself. 'Just enough wind to make it a real race, and what a superb setting!' She indicated the island-sprinkled gulf, then shook her head at the man beside her. 'Nick, why on earth haven't you told me about this fabulous place?'

Cat wondered spitefully what Nick heard when Francesca said his name, and was immediately ashamed of herself.

At that moment a gun was fired, and the three long, sleekly graceful millionaires' toys surged across a start line.

It didn't matter that Cat knew little about yacht racing; a fugitive happiness settled in her heart. Nobody, she thought, sitting on the deck with Nick beside her, nobody and nothing could take this moment, this precious joy, away from her.

When it was over, and the winner cheered, the flotilla sailed into a bay on Kawau Island and anchored there.

The party was held in the garden area in front of a large, Victorian house, once the home of a long-dead Governor of New Zealand. Judging by the plants he'd collected he'd been something of an amateur botanist; as dusk fell each magnificent specimen on the lawn behind the beach glittered with fairy lights. To the noise of anchor chains rattling down, people still scurried in and out of the marquee on last-minute chores, and the air was filled with the potent miasma of party-goers determined to enjoy themselves.

Cat donned her other evening dress, a blue georgette shift that skimmed her body lightly and showed off her shoulders and the gentle curves of her breasts. She peered through the porthole and noted that some paths were concrete, and some gravel. The slim-heeled sandals she'd chosen would deal with both, although she'd have to take them off if she decided to wander along the beach. This time she wore no jewellery but the Tanzanite ring.

Others had not been so circumspect. Most women—and a few of the men—positively gleamed with jewellery. Everyone had pulled out all the stops, dazzling with clothes and gems straight from the pages of glossy magazines.

But designer outfits and important jewellery, the big silk marquee, even the splendid yachts in the bay, couldn't overwhelm the magnificent seascape, that magical, haunting combination of land and sea that made hardened travellers exclaim with delight.

As he had all day, Nick kept her close by him, but after dinner he was approached by a man whose face she recalled from the previous night's party.

'Mr Penn would like to know something about the history of the gardens,' he said politely, and added, 'He was most impressed with the conversation you had with him last night.'

Which, unless Cat was reading things entirely wrong, meant that the so-important and powerful Mr Penn wanted to discuss something with Nick. Because Mr Penn was confined to a wheelchair he conducted his socialising rather like a royal audience.

When Nick hesitated, Cat said cheerfully, 'I could do

with some quiet. I'll go and sit underneath that massive Moreton Bay fig tree on the beach.'

'I'll be back as soon as I can,' Nick said.

Cat nodded, smiled at Mr Penn's attendant, and wandered across to the tree. Some intelligent and thoughtful person had placed chairs beneath the immense swooping branches, but they were empty.

More than happy to be alone, watching the moon silver the waters of the bay, Cat sat down.

Movement caught her eye. The lights glimmered on dark hair, a slender body clad in black. Although Cat had only seen her twice before, she knew instantly who she was— Morna Vause, Nick's childhood friend, who'd designed her ring and the pearl necklace.

'Hello, Cathy,' Morna drawled. Something about her slightly unfocused gaze made Cat wonder if she'd had too much champagne. 'So we meet once more.'

'Nice to see you again,' Cat said carefully and inanely.

Smiling with an irony that Cat felt was deserved, Morna Vause sat down, a long glass clutched in both hands. 'The ring looks great; balanced. Buyers often don't realise that designs should suit the people who wear them. When Nick commissioned the pearls I chose medium-sized ones with the finest orient—lustre—I could lay my hands on. I could have used ones the size of pigeon's eggs, but they'd have drowned your face.'

Cat looked down at the exquisite ring that had come to symbolise all that was sham about her relationship with Nick. 'You're a genius.'

'Not quite.' The wide, sultry mouth twisted. 'I knew all about you, you see.'

Something wasn't right. The unease that had tingled through Cat when she'd first seen the woman roared back.

'I suppose Nick described me,' she said, because Morna was waiting for an answer.

'I already knew what you looked like. Friends—' she made the word sound like an insult '—sent me photographs of your wedding, so I knew you were small and delicate and beautiful. And young.'

Cat's lips felt stiff. 'I'm afraid I don't—'

'We never met until Nick brought you to the showroom because when Glen decided you'd make the perfect wife for him he packed me off overseas so that I wouldn't cause trouble.'

'What?' Cat froze.

Morna's laugh was cracked and unsteady. 'It still astonishes me that no one told you, or that you didn't guess. You must have gone around with your eyes closed and your ears shut. Our break-up was the biggest thing in Auckland since the Ark hit Ararat,' she said sarcastically. Lifting her glass, she gulped from it before saying with dogged precision, 'I wonder what it is about you that men find so bloody irresistible.' She gave another harsh laugh. 'No, I know what it is. Beauty is so unfair and men are such fools.'

Very quietly Cat said, 'This is not the place for this conversation.' Yet the woman's white face and air of febrile determination proclaimed that Morna wouldn't be put off.

Something Sister Bernadette had once said to Cat flashed into her mind. Cat had just got up from tending to a woman who'd wept for the loss of her whole family, murdered by insurgents at the height of the war.

When at last the woman had sunk into unconsciousness, Cat had said bitterly, 'I wish I could do something for her! I can't formulate the words to help her. All I can do is hold her hand and make her comfortable, and that's so completely useless...'

In her broad Australian accent the nun had said briskly, 'That's all anyone can do—let her spill it out. People want an ear to listen, to ease the burden a little. Do that, and you've helped more than you'll ever guess.'

She could do this for Nick's friend—just listen.

'Not the place for a conversation like this?' Morna mimicked, and laughed. 'Tough. I'm not likely to have another chance to get close to you; Nick guards you like a gaoler. If he never speaks to me again I'm going to get this off my chest. Of course he blames himself because he introduced me to Glen. I fell in love with him and he loved me. We lived together for five years. I thought we were going to do the whole thing—marriage, kids, happy ever after— all the stuff we women aren't supposed to want any more because a career is better.'

Such pain jagged through her voice that Cat covered the long, strong fingers on the table with her own hand.

Snatching her hand away, Morna whispered, 'Don't you dare feel sorry for me!' She dragged in a deep, gasping breath. 'But Glen didn't want that with me. He met you— sweet and innocent and charmingly yielding, too young to know anything—and before I knew what had happened he'd organised me off to New York. Oh, it was the chance of a lifetime—I studied in the best design studios—but it was still the traditional kiss-off.'

'I didn't know,' Cat said rigidly, although now remembered innuendoes, sly glances, remarks cut short echoed inside her head. How stupidly blind she'd been!

'I asked him why,' Morna said. 'I wanted him to come out and say why he was dumping me. He didn't. So I told him. He couldn't cope with competition; he was so insecure he surrounded himself with young people because they admired him and supported him.'

Yes, she did understand him, far better than Cat had. Cat

frowned, but before she could say anything Morna swept on, 'That's what he wanted in a wife—someone demure and gentle and malleable—someone who was all the things I wasn't.'

'I know,' Cat said. And when the girl he'd chosen had turned out to be not quite as obedient as he'd expected— when she'd insisted on going to university—he'd petulantly embarked on an affair.

Morna shrugged. 'He wasn't hard to read, my poor Glen. At least Nick stood by me. He told Glen exactly what he thought of him.' She set her glass down on the table with a ringing crack, then snatched it up again. 'Glen was so taken aback he gobbled like a turkey, but Nick took no notice of him. He left Glen for me, looked after me, flew to New York when I was down—' She leaned forward, the glass slipping sideways to spill a little of its contents. Intensely she said, 'His loyalty saved my life. If it hadn't been for him I'd have killed myself.'

'I'm so sorry.' Cat tried to forget that when Glen died she'd had no one.

No, that wasn't true; she'd had friends.

Morna stared at her. 'Yes, I think you are,' she said at last. A small, gloating smile curved her mouth. 'I've been watching you. You're trying to hide it, but you're in love with Nick. I hope you don't think he loves you. He's enjoying you, but he'll never be comfortable sleeping with Glen's wife. Loyalty's a two-edged sword, and Nick is loyal both to me and to Glen.' Her smile contorted into a grimace. 'Perhaps when he leaves you we can get together and swap stories on how betrayal feels, how it tastes, how it darkens your life.'

'He won't betray me,' Cat said steadily, because she wouldn't let him. She'd accepted the end of their affair before it had started; she'd go with dignity. Pride was about the only thing she had left, but it would keep her upright.

'Perhaps it's that innocent, trusting naïvety that gets them,' Morna remarked, an odd inflection in her voice. 'Well, innocence won't last with Nick—he's an education in sophistication. Basically he doesn't trust women. Except me, of course, and he's not going to trust me any more when he finds out I've told you all this.'

Cat said, 'He doesn't need to know.'

The older woman ignored her. 'Do you know why he doesn't trust women? His mother abandoned him when he was seven; he came home from school one day and she'd gone. A new family had shifted in. He just stood there, his face totally blank.'

'Oh, God,' Cat breathed, horror making her feel sick. She knew that look.

'Her new boyfriend didn't want Nick, so she left him behind like an old sock. My mother took him in.' Morna laughed angrily. 'Not that living with us was much improvement.'

'Your mother must have been kind,' Cat pointed out.

'Only because it took less effort than being angry,' Morna said bluntly. 'She watched television all day because she had no money and no dreams. We kids brought ourselves up. But Nick and I always knew we wanted more—soon it was him and me against the world. I could rely on him, and he could rely on me. When he'd earned enough money he got me an apprenticeship at a jeweller's. And when Glen dumped me he left him and went out on his own.'

'I see,' Cat said tonelessly, wondering if this was the real reason that Nick broke his ties with Glen.

'I hated you for years. Why do we hate the person who supplants us, not the one who does the dumping?' Morna shrugged. 'Human nature, I suppose. Oddly enough, I don't hate you now, and I think I might even be able to forgive Glen.'

Gently Cat said, 'I'm very sorry that you've had such a tough time, and I'm glad Nick was there for you.'

'You think I'm unstable, wallowing in self-pity, don't you?' She overrode Cat's protest. 'See how you feel when Nick leaves you—and believe me, he'll do it. He won't ever let another woman abandon him like his mother did— he gets out first. However much he wants you, whatever spell you've cast over him, he's strong enough to cut you out of his life, and he will.' Morna drained her glass and set it down with exaggerated care. 'What I'd really like to know is why the two hardest-headed men I've known lost their heads over you. You're certainly not the standard dolly-bird.'

'I'll take that as a compliment,' Cat said drily, wondering if there was any way she could help Morna. Just listening didn't seem to be accomplishing anything, yet she didn't know her well enough to do anything more.

'Actually,' Morna said abruptly, 'I feel better. It's been like—oh, letting the pressure off.'

To Cat's astonishment the other woman's eyes sheened with tears. 'Hi,' she said with a shaky smile, looking past Cat.

Nick. Cat swivelled, to be greeted by such a blaze of fury that she felt sick. 'What's going on here?' Nick demanded.

'It's all right,' Morna said uneasily. 'We've just been talking, haven't we, Cathy?'

A swift agitation gripped Cat, because after that first furious glance Nick strode around the table and held out his hand to Morna. 'What boat are you on?'

'The *Seamew*. Lolly Applegate's ketch.'

'I'll take you back.'

He looped an arm over her shoulder, pulling her gently to her feet. Without looking at Cat, Morna rose gracefully. 'I'm all right,' she said wearily. 'In fact, I feel better. Empty, but a good emptiness.'

Nick looked at Cat. 'Do you mind if I see Morna—?'

'Of course not,' she broke in automatically.

His eyes narrowed, but he smiled at the woman standing beside him and said, 'Come on.'

Cat's heart began to beat heavily, slowly, as she watched them walk away. Although there was nothing sexual about the way Nick looked at Morna, spoke to her, touched her, there was affection and liking, and a tenderness he'd never shown Cat.

That tenderness hurt more than anything else in her life. All of her dreams had been based on folly, and the knowledge was like a knife to her heart, so painful that she literally couldn't breathe.

'Bit rude that, going off with another woman!'

Even before she registered the intruder's presence, Cat recognised the English accent. She pinned a cool smile to her lips as Julian Forrester sat down and smiled at her, his bold eyes making no secret of his appreciation.

'It's a fantastic party, isn't it?' she said warily.

Grinning, he leaned forward. 'Better now that I've seen you. Would you like another drink?'

'No, thank you.' He might make her uncomfortable, but only Nick could hurt or intimidate her.

'I've been watching you, trying to work out why you don't fit in,' he said. 'In the end I realised it was that patrician face. I can always tell good breeding.'

Cat's brows rose. 'Really?' His words made her feel rather like a prize animal, and so did the glance that went with them.

He smiled complacently. 'A thoroughbred through and through.' His eyes swept the guests with more than a hint of disdain. 'You stand out in this bunch of *nouveau riche* upstarts like a flower in a field of thistles.'

Cat wondered whether this heavy-handed approach to flirtation ever worked. Possibly with someone completely lacking in self-confidence.

She returned crisply, 'These "*nouveau riche* upstarts" have worked incredibly hard to get where they are. Most people would consider that a more worthy character trait than relying on good breeding—which usually means that one's distant ancestors did all the hard work.' She added, 'And it shows a total *lack* of breeding to criticise the people whose hospitality you're accepting.' Her eyes rested thoughtfully on his glass, then flicked up to his chagrined face as she got to her feet.

His hand shot out and fastened with surprising strength around her wrist. 'No, you don't,' he said in a thickened voice. 'Who the hell do you think you are? You're just one of the whores who hang around anyone with a million or so in the hopes of earning some of it on your back. You can sit down and pretend you like me, or I'll see that your present owner misses out on the deal he's trying to stitch together.'

'You don't know what you're talking about.'

His laugh came close to a snarl. 'I know. In fact, if you don't change your attitude very quickly, I might suggest that if he wants the deal to go ahead he lends you to me for a while. He might have money but I've got the contacts, and if I apply a bit of pressure—' his fingers tightened painfully around her wrist '—his precious new project will go down the drain.'

'You are incredibly vulgar,' she said, hiding nausea with scorn, and planning the sudden jerk that would free her.

'But you like your men vulgar, or you wouldn't be sleeping with one who grew up on the streets,' he said maliciously. 'Unless, of course, you like money more than civilised behaviour.'

Cat said distantly, 'Let me go.'

'When you sit down again.'

'Let her go.' Nick's voice—so lethal that the hairs on the back of Cat's neck stood up in the age-old response to a threat.

She wasn't surprised when the man who held her dropped her wrist as though it had suddenly become redhot.

Scrambling to his feet, he tried for his usual tone of clipped self-satisfaction. 'Steady on, there.'

Nick ignored him to reach out and take Cat's hand. He didn't say anything, but his anger burned with the intensity of a dark flame when he examined the red fingermarks on her skin.

She said sharply, 'No.'

He raised his head and looked at her for the first time, and she almost cried out at the stark fury flaming dangerously in his golden eyes. 'No, what?' he asked in that silken, coldly reckless tone.

She shrugged. 'He's not worth it,' she said, struggling to speak calmly. 'Trash is dirty; that's just how it is.'

Nick smiled and lifted her hand, holding it against his mouth for a long second. Before Cat had done more than draw in a sharp, impeded breath, he let her go and he looked at the man who stood across the table, his squared shoulders and arrogantly high head failing to conceal his fundamental uneasiness.

Like that he seemed a poor creature, shifty, suddenly sleazy. With slicing contempt Nick said softly, 'Listen to me, Forrester. If I ever see you within ten feet of her again I'll give you what you've been asking for.'

'Oh, I realise I can't match you for size,' the other man sneered, 'but I'm not afraid of you.'

Nick laughed with real, chilling amusement. 'I don't fight men who aren't up to my weight,' he said. 'Your face is safe. But your company is not.'

Julian Forrester stared at him, his cheeks fading to a pasty white. He licked his lips. 'What the hell has my company got to do with this?'

'Annoy my woman with your attentions again, and you'll see. I might not want to soil my hands by hitting you, but I certainly won't waste a moment's regret when I bankrupt you.' Nick said it negligently, but only a stupid person would assume that he didn't mean every word.

'Over a woman?' Julian Forrester was incredulous, his eyes darting from Cat's appalled face to Nick's. 'Hell, man, why quarrel over a little—'

'That's enough.' Nick's voice cracked like a whip. His fingers closed again on Cat's, tucked her hand into his arm. 'Get out of my sight,' he said with uncompromising force-fulness.

Julian Forrester stared at him. Cat recognised the moment the tightly leashed fury in Nick's cold, autocratic face finally cut through the cocoon of his conceit. 'I always thought that whatever else you lacked, you had brains,' he said contemptuously when he was beyond Nick's reach, 'but I see I was mistaken.'

In spite of the malice of his final words, his departure resembled the desperate strut of a defeated opponent deter-mined to salvage what small amount of self-respect he could from a bruising encounter.

Watching him, Cat said urgently, 'He said he could make trouble for you in some deal.'

'He hasn't got a hope, the little worm.' Although Nick sounded supremely confident, his black fury still rode him. Casting a swift, impatient glance around, he said abruptly, 'I need to talk to you.'

'All right,' Cat said, weariness draining her of strength.

But Francesca intercepted them. 'Nick, one of the stewards from the yacht was looking for you—apparently someone's trying to contact you urgently,' she said, light winking and gleaming on the diamond studs in her ears, the diamond-encrusted chain around her long golden throat.

'It's all right—I've got the message,' Nick told her.

'Bad news?' Francesca asked, her gaze going from Nick's grave face to Cat's astonished one.

He put his warm hand over Cat's, holding her anchored by his side. 'Not good.'

Francesca hesitated before saying, 'Do you want me to come back to the boat with you?'

'No,' Nick said, 'we'll be all right.'

She nodded and said soberly, 'Let me know if there's anything I can do. The tender's waiting for you at the wharf.'

As Nick urged Cat towards the wharf she demanded urgently, 'What's going on?'

'My PA forwarded a message to the yacht,' he told her, his voice calm and controlled. 'It's from the hospital in Romit. They couldn't reach you, so they very sensibly got through to me. Because the message was urgent, the master of the yacht sent it ashore.'

The colour drained from her skin. 'I forgot to tell them I'd moved,' she said woodenly. Because all she'd been thinking of was living with Nick. She swallowed to ease her dry throat and asked huskily, 'Is it Juana?'

'I'm afraid it is.' Fairy lights twinkled across his grim face, revealing only too clearly that what he had to tell her was bad news. 'She's contracted a bacterial infection. They've done what they can, but she needs specialised hospital care in Australia.'

Cat bit her lip so hard he saw a tiny bead of blood ooze forth. However, she said in a brisk, cool voice, 'I'll get back to them and tell them to put her on the next plane.'

'I've already organised it. She should be leaving Ilid in half an hour.'

Cat looked up at him, her face revealing such naked emotion that he felt a raw, humiliating jealousy. In a voice choked with gratitude she said, 'Thank you.'

Nick wondered why her transparent relief grated so harshly on him.

It was, he thought, characteristic that she'd abandon this exclusive gathering because of one small child. He'd watched her as she moved amongst the wealthy and powerful at his side; she'd responded to them all with a generous interest enhanced by the excellent manners drilled into her by her parents.

Yet although she clearly appreciated the good things money could buy, she didn't seem particularly impressed by it, possibly because she had more than her fair share of strength, will-power and sheer, gritty stubbornness.

Somehow her determination to do what she could for the child had infected him too, but he intended to make sure those who ran the clinic weren't taking advantage of Cat's sense of responsibility.

She was alone in the world, which had to be why he suffered this inconvenient protectiveness.

He smiled inwardly, mocking himself. Who was he trying to fool? These past days had taught him what his thick head had refused to accept for years—after one look at Cat, nothing had ever been the same again.

Cat interrupted his thoughts with a question. 'Is Morna all right?'

'What did you say to her?' he asked.

Cat withdrew her hand from his arm. 'Nothing much,' she said remotely. 'I just listened. That's what you do when someone is compelled to spill their heart. I think she'd been bottling everything up inside ever since Glen—'

'Dumped her,' he supplied with brutal honesty when she hesitated. He went on, 'Whatever you did or didn't do, it seemed to work. For the past six years she's been a driven woman—frantically busy socially, and taking on far too much work. Tonight when I walked her back she seemed different, almost peaceful, as though talking to you helped her to finally put Glen behind her.'

'I hope so,' Cat said in a muted voice. 'He wasn't worth all that pain.' Her voice hardened. 'No man is worth so much pain! Why didn't you tell me what Glen had done?'

'Watch your step!' The concrete changed into gravel beneath their feet. Cat's high heels looked dangerous and fragile, but she walked with her usual grace over the loose stone chippings.

Nick dragged his eyes away from her slender legs and ankles. 'Because it wasn't my secret.'

'No wonder you hated me.'

'That had nothing to do with the way I felt about you. Glen betrayed her—you didn't.'

And because he didn't want to talk about this any longer, he asked abruptly, 'Would you like to fly across to see Juana?'

She gave him an uncertain glance. 'I promised to stay with you,' she said quietly. 'Besides, Juana won't know me now—she'll get on fine as long as Rosita's there. And the nuns will have organised someone to look after them both while they're in Australia.'

But he could see she wanted to go. As they reached the man who waited for them by the yacht tender, he made up his mind. 'Get the stewardess to pack our clothes,' he said. 'I'll organise the flight. Have you got your passport with you?'

'Yes. But, Nick—'

'What's your problem?'

She shook her head. 'No problem. I'm just surprised that what I want matters,' she said with an edge to her voice. 'It hasn't before.'

The calm, mysterious silver of the moon glimmered in her eyes, picking out with slumbrous clarity the lush curves of her mouth, the smooth sinuous line of her throat and gentle swell of her breasts. Sudden, primal lust twisted inside him, urgent, demanding.

'It always mattered,' he said, his voice tight and thick.

He wanted a lonely beach and six months with this woman, and possibly then he'd get her out of his system, become his own man again.

Sleeping with her hadn't done it; perhaps he should suggest a more prosaic, more financial arrangement than this half-fantasy relationship. Mistress was an old-fashioned term, but surely familiarity would eventually breed boredom?

Desperation clawed him; from the time he'd met Cat he'd been confronted by emotions he couldn't control, emotions too primitive to be trusted. He'd never thought he'd fall in love, but if this wasn't love it had to be obsession—either way it was dangerous because it threatened the independence he'd worked so hard to acquire.

'Hurry up,' he said curtly, 'or we'll miss the plane.'

CHAPTER ELEVEN

BUT the small executive jet was waiting for them at Auckland airport. Cat collapsed into a luxurious seat, exhausted as though she'd been caught in a hurricane that had whirled her away from the glamour of the party and into reality—a reality where defenceless, innocent children died because they had the misfortune to be born at the wrong time in the wrong place.

Except, she thought wryly, that this wasn't real life yet. She looked around the empty cabin of the aircraft and asked as they left the ground, 'Who does this belong to?'

'Stan,' Nick said briefly.

He'd been almost silent since that last astonishing comment on the island. Cat looked up at his profile, clear-cut and as uncompromising as steel. What had he meant by it? Too cowardly to ask, she said, 'It was nice of him to offer it.'

'Yes.'

Something in Nick's tone caught her attention. 'He didn't offer it, did he? You chartered it.'

'Both,' Nick said without expression. 'He offered and I chartered. I'll get the stewardess to make up the bed once this levels out. In the meantime, try to relax—you're wound tight as a spring.'

Obediently Cat leaned back, but nothing could block the image of Juana, deathly ill and even now flying towards the hospital that would save her, please God.

Eventually, by strenuously convincing herself that fretting helped nobody, she managed to sidestep that and ponder Francesca's last words.

Their hostess had arrived back on board just before they'd left for Auckland. Nick had been speaking to the yacht's master while Cat stood in the saloon amid a waste of white leather and stared out over the sea, black and glossy beneath the impersonal moon, the hills of the mainland sharp cut-outs against a luminous sky.

'Good luck,' Francesca had said. 'For the little girl, I mean. I don't think *you* need any. I suppose I knew I was on a losing wicket that first day when I walked into Nick's house and saw that it was decorated to match you.'

Cat had swung around to stare at her.

The other woman had given a little laugh. 'Don't tell me you didn't notice? You don't deserve him, you know. Blue the same colour as your eyes, touches of chestnut, and creamy-white to match your skin. Were you and Nick lovers before your husband died?'

'No.'

'But he already loved you.'

'No,' Cat had said quietly, her heart compressing in pain. The only thing between her and Nick was a reluctant, obsessive passion.

Francesca had been watching her with a faint frown. 'I believe you,' she'd said unexpectedly. 'Don't other people?'

'Other people don't matter,' Cat had said quietly.

Shrugging, Francesca had bestowed an ironic smile on her. 'Hmm, no doubt I'd think that too if Nick wanted me. And perhaps you do need some of that good luck after all— I doubt if he's an easy man to love.'

Now, with the whine of the jets a kind of lullaby, Cat thought achingly that Francesca was wrong—in spite of her best efforts not to, Cat had found it so easy to love Nick.

And surely it was pure coincidence that the colours he'd used in his house were her colours? Yes, it had to be, because the house had been decorated by a professional.

Tiny, valiant, Juana lay in a small isolation ward in the Tropical Medicine unit of a big Queensland hospital. Black hair spiky with sweat against the pillow, she had an oxygen mask covering her face and her eyelids were closed and swollen. Beside her bed crouched her aunt, weeping. A nurse did something with a drip.

'Rosita,' Cat breathed, dread catching her heart. She ran across and slipped her arms around the girl, holding her as she said in her halting Romitese, 'Don't cry, don't cry.'

But Rosita whispered, 'See, she is sweating, not burning up with fire, and the disease is dying. She smiled at me! Soon she will be hungry! She will be well in a few days, the doctor said. It is a miracle.' She knuckled away her tears and repeated, 'She will be well,' as though it was a mantra.

'Once we found out what the bug was, we knew what antibiotic to give her,' the nurse said with an appreciative glance at Nick. 'She's responded spectacularly.'

Cat breathed, 'Oh, thank God. Rosita, this is Nick Harding,' she said hastily when the girl looked past her. 'He brought me over from New Zealand.' Switching to English, she said, 'Nick, this is Rosita.'

Rosita put her hands together and bowed, as she'd been taught in some distant, happy childhood before the war, and then held out her hand. Her small brown paw locked in Nick's, she used up almost her entire stock of English. 'How do you do?'

'How do you do, Rosita?' he said formally, and smiled at her.

Shyly, radiantly, Rosita smiled back.

Yet another victim to his potent charm, Cat thought with resignation, turning away to lean over the bed and whisper Juana's name. Slowly the dark eyes opened; beneath the oxygen mask Juana's scarred mouth smiled and she held out a thin little hand.

Tears clogging Cat's throat, she bent to kiss the baby's brow. Juana's fingers tangled in chestnut hair, then fell away, and she went back to sleep again with the startling suddenness of the very young.

Cat straightened up and met Nick's eyes. He was gazing at her as though he'd never seen her before, his face completely impassive, eyes blank. He looked, she thought wonderingly, like someone who'd just received a body-blow— like the small boy who'd come home from school to face the end of his world.

A bustle at the door heralded a doctor, and when Cat glanced again at Nick he was himself again, in charge, confident.

Perhaps she'd imagined that moment, that look. Yet as the day unfolded she sensed that something had driven Nick behind the formidable barricades she knew so well. Their intimacy of the past days had vanished, blasted away by his will-power and self-control.

Later the doctor told them that barring relapses Juana should be out of hospital by the end of the week, and asked whether they had planned to do anything about the surgery she needed.

'That's all arranged,' Nick said. 'As soon as the child's well enough she'll be operated on by Mr Geddy.'

The doctor's reverent expression established that Mr Geddy was a miracle-worker. 'You couldn't do better,' he said heartily.

Nick went on, 'Ms Courtald will stay here, and take

Rosita and Juana back to Romit when the child's convalescence is over.'

Discreetly ignoring Cat's astonishment, the doctor said smoothly, 'That sounds ideal.'

Back at the hotel they'd checked into that morning, Cat said, 'Thank you for organising everything.'

'It was the least I could do,' Nick said calmly. 'Tomorrow you and Rosita will move into an apartment—I thought you'd prefer that to a hotel.'

'I can't afford—'

'It's the one I use when I come here,' he said impassively. 'I've opened a bank account and put in the other half of the money I owe you, as well as a sum that should cover expenses while you're here. If you need more, ring me.'

Cat bit her lip. 'I'll be sensible with it,' she said stonily.

His expression didn't alter. 'Your tickets to Romit have been paid for; activate them when you want to go.' His tone warned her not to object. 'Get in touch with me if anything goes wrong.'

Pain clenched Cat's heart. 'When are you going back?'

He paused, then said, 'Now.'

Don't make a scene, she told herself. She lifted her chin and even managed to smile. 'Thank you. I should tell you I don't need your money, but I'll have to use it. I'll pay you back, I promise.'

'I don't want any repayment,' he said curtly.

'You might not,' she returned, 'but you're going to get it.' She held out her hand, vaguely pleased to see that it didn't shake. 'Then—good luck, Nick.'

He took, it, looked down at it with something like a frown. 'Good luck,' he said.

And pulled her into his arms and kissed her as though it

was the last thing he would ever do on this earth, as though his sole chance of heaven lay in the touch of her mouth.

Cat went up like wildfire, desire storming through her to meet the desperate hunger of that kiss.

Yet almost immediately he lifted his head and dropped his arms. She gazed into hard, crystalline eyes as he said harshly, 'Take care of yourself.'

As the door closed behind him she thought dully that Morna was right. He'd never let himself lose control and fall in love with her, and he'd never give her the chance to reject him again.

She didn't cry, not then nor during the long weeks as Juana recovered from her illness before returning to hospital for reconstructive surgery. Cat discovered that it was possible to live a normal life and convince those who cared about you that everything was fine when your heart lay in painful shards inside you.

She even managed to reach some sort of equilibrium, although every tall dark man she saw rubbed raw her profound, bitter yearning. She dreamed, and woke to heartache, but she carried on because Rosita and Juana needed her.

At last came the day when they flew into Ilid. From the air it was obvious that the little city was still ravaged by war, although there were signs of rebuilding. The airport conducted its business in temporary shelters, and most of the planes that used the strip were military ones from the peace-keeping force.

'Sister Bernadette,' Cat cried, shifting Juana to her hip as the heat settled on them like a thick, moist cloak. 'Oh, everyone's here! How lovely to see you all!'

The nun laughed. 'Welcome back.'

A crowd surrounded them, familiar faces from the village by the clinic. Choked by sudden tears, Cat handed Juana to Rosita. While in Australia they had shopped for the little girl, and for her homecoming they'd dressed Juana in an exquisite little white dress, ruffled and embroidered, with a sunbonnet and small white shoes and socks.

The greetings were prolonged and noisy; Juana was passed from admiring arms to admiring arms, all exclaiming over her beauty and health, until Sister Bernadette shepherded them outside, saying briskly, 'Come on, we have to collect some goods from the inward depot and then we'll go home.'

Cat stopped. 'You've got another truck!' The battered old one had blown up on a landmine just before Cat had left Romit. This one was bigger and had clearly been new when it arrived at the clinic, although the island's red dust already lay thickly over the paintwork. 'Goodness,' she said, 'this is very smart!'

Sister Bernadette said drily, 'Much more suitable than our old banger. I'm glad you approve because some of your money went towards it. You and Rosita and Juana sit in the front with me,' she commanded, 'and everyone else on the back. Keep your arms inside!'

Cat planned to stay a week, although she knew she was putting off the time when she'd have to go back to New Zealand—back to reality. She had to find a job and a place to live; she had to make herself a life—a life finally and irrevocably without Nick.

They'd communicated briefly, in absurdly formal words. Once she was back she'd cut the connection; she couldn't bear this long-drawn-out purgatory.

Halfway through the week she walked along the wide veranda of the clinic, waving at a group of urchins who were playing in the shade of a huge rain tree.

'Cat.'

At first she thought she was hallucinating. Heart jumping

in absurd hope, she turned, and saw Nick walking towards her, accompanied by Sister Bernadette. If this was a hallucination, it was also visual, and very sturdy.

'What are you doing here?' she asked shakily.

Sister Bernadette said, 'He came to check us out.'

Cat looked from her amused face to Nick's, violently compelling, the dark skin a little drawn. He looked as though he'd lost weight, she thought painfully. 'Check us out?' she repeated, transferring her gaze back at the nun in case he discerned the joy that raced through her.

'He wanted to make sure that we weren't an evil institution bleeding you dry.'

Cat's gaze flew to Nick. 'You did what—?'

'I'm glad he did,' Sister Bernadette interrupted forthrightly. 'Your heart's too big—you need a sensible financial type to oversee your interests. Now, I have work to do, and I know you have a lot to talk about, so I'll leave you.'

Cat hardly noticed her departure. Anger and a fierce pleasure sizzled through her, restoring her to life. 'You had no right to spy on them,' she said fiercely.

'Are we always going to fight?' he asked blandly, lifting his brows. 'Yes, we probably will. I'll do what I think is necessary, and you'll object.'

Cat stared at him. 'What are you talking about?'

'Have you missed me?'

When she didn't answer, he went on, 'I hope you have, because I've missed you.' His voice deepened. 'Unbearably, Cat. I've spent nights aching for you, and days when the only thing that saved me was knowing that I'd see you soon.'

Her mouth trembled. She put out a hand and clung to the railing of the veranda. 'It's no use. I can't—*won't*—go through that again.'

He said, 'Why not?'

'Because I'm not a masochist!' she snapped.

Laughing deep in his throat, he tilted her chin so that he could look into her eyes. His flashed gold, all arrogance gone, its place taken by a rare humility. 'Years ago Glen told me that only fools put all their eggs in one basket. It's true, but where you're concerned I've done just that. These past weeks have been hell, because life without you is a desert.' His thumb traced the shape of her mouth. In a voice that had turned grim, he asked, 'I have to know if it's been a desert for you too.'

She said quietly, 'Of course it has. But that's not enough, is it? You'll never forgive yourself for wanting me when I belonged to Glen.'

The arrogant framework of his face stood out sharply. 'You never belonged to Glen.' Dropping his hand, he turned away and walked across to the rough wooden balustrade. Without looking at her he said, 'But for years I tried to convince myself that I reacted so violently to you because I felt guilty.'

'*I* certainly felt guilty.'

Nick rested his hands on the railing of the veranda, leaning on them to stare out across the compound. Against a background of childish shrieks he said with clinical detachment, 'Right from the start I knew I could have you, and that if we made love, you'd cancel the wedding. I told myself that it was loyalty to Glen that stopped me from taking you to bed.'

Cat's breath locked in her throat.

Keeping his face averted so that she could only see his profile, angular, granite-hard against the setting sun, he went on in the same dispassionate voice, 'It was enough of the truth to convince me, but it wasn't the whole truth.'

Cat swallowed. 'And what is the whole truth?' she asked.

His knuckles tightened on the balustrade. 'There's no logic to it, but even at that first meeting I knew that you were my other half, the one woman in all the world who was made for me, the reason I was born.'

'If you'd told me that when you asked me to cancel the wedding, I'd almost certainly have done it,' she whispered, not daring to let the tiny flicker of hope burn into a flame.

He gave a hard, ironic laugh. 'That's why I didn't say it, because you thought you loved Glen. And because I couldn't offer you anything to take his place. You weren't ready to marry anyone then. You needed time to grow up.'

'You knew me better than I knew myself,' she said sadly.

'Neither of us was very self-aware,' he said with irony. 'I've always been suspicious of emotions and prided myself on my clear thinking. Six years ago the last thing I'd have admitted to was some mystical link with a girl I scarcely knew! And I've gone on refusing to admit it until a week or so ago, when Morna told me that I'd never really coped with what my mother did.' He paused. 'She said she'd told you about my mother's somewhat abrupt departure from my life.'

Something about the cool deliberation in his tone set Cat's temper alight. She could see him—a small, handsome boy, standing at his house door and seeing strangers there. 'It made me feel sick,' she said angrily.

He turned his head for a moment and smiled. 'My fierce, tender-hearted Cat! It wasn't the first time Morna had accused me of blindness where women were concerned, but this time it hit home. I suppose I've always measured women by my mother—not consciously, but when I examined my motivation I realised that I've seen you through a distorting glass.'

Cat said quietly, 'That's understandable.'

'I don't think so. I should have seen that you were nothing like my mother, yet when you came to me for help I tested you by putting that degrading proposition to you, and when you agreed I wondered whether you wanted another husband who could give you security.'

'Oh, did you?' she asked ominously.

'Yes,' he said with a self-mocking smile. 'But living with you was hell. I soon realised that you weren't mercenary, and when you left the party without hesitation to go to a child you felt responsible for, I knew that I'd read you entirely wrong. And that's when I realised that I hadn't dared claim you before you married Glen because I was afraid you'd reject me.'

'Oh, *Nick*,' she said, heartbroken for him, wishing she could take away that old, deep-seated pain.

'Amazing how blind I was. Even though I kissed you in anger, I still hoped you'd give Glen up. Instead, you went ahead and married him.'

A raw note in his voice twisted her heart. Painfully she said, 'It was only a day before the wedding; three hundred people had been invited! I know it sounds stupid now, but I just couldn't face it. Everybody would have wanted to know why, and I didn't have a reason. One kiss is not enough reason to shatter lives, to cause so much unhappiness. The last four years of my mother's life were serene because I married Glen.'

Nick laughed without humour, a fierce, cynical sound that made her shiver in the humid, tropical afternoon. 'And that makes it worthwhile? In other words, you opted for security.'

The sun was just about to set behind the rim of the jungle; soon dusk would race across the compound. The declining sun laid a wash of light across Nick's face, transforming him into a bronze god from some ancient, primitive era—ruthless, demanding, intolerant.

Anguished desire kicked Cat in the heart. 'In every way. I was a kid, I hadn't even had a crush on anyone, and you stormed into my life, dark and dangerous and utterly overwhelming! Women watched you out of the corner of their eyes, and made little noises in their throats when they talked about you. Of course I thought Glen was safer! I thought I loved him—I was sure my reaction to you was wildly abnormal, because I know that love at first sight is a myth and I didn't know you at all.'

Nick said, 'Standing beside him in that bloody church and listening to you saying your vows gave me the final impetus to leave the life he'd mapped out for me. I was determined to make a fortune so that I could fling it in your face.'

He paused, then said with brutal self-contempt, 'Though really I wanted to lay it at your feet. I was a coward. I hoped you'd break the engagement so that I wouldn't be the one to betray Glen, yet I knew that just looking at you the way I did, feeling this overwhelming hunger—was a betrayal. And you were so young, not ready for the kind of passion I felt.'

Aching for the years they'd wasted—and still miserably aware that he'd said nothing about love—Cat said, 'Six years ago you weren't that old yourself, Nick.'

'Old enough to understand that whatever had happened between us was—special,' he said. 'Afterwards I tried everything to get over what I decided was a highly suspicious obsession. I drove myself almost into the ground, made love to other women, tried so hard to forget you I fooled myself into thinking I'd done it—only to realise when you walked into my office in Auckland and demanded money from me—'

'I didn't demand!'

He laughed softly. 'You threw your request in my teeth. It was a direct challenge—and I realised that everything I'd done to prise you out of my heart had been for nothing, that I'd been waiting for you to come to me. I wanted to shackle you to my side, even though I still wouldn't accept that it was anything more than a reluctant, particularly ruthless passion.' He gave a taut smile. 'I even bought the picture for my office because the woman in it had hair and skin the colour of yours.'

From across the compound came the sounds of children laughing, the whisper of an evening wind in the palms. The monsoon rains were a distant memory and the red dust in the compound stirred sluggishly, then sank back onto the unpaved ground.

Did he mean that he felt more for her than that reluctant obsession? Cautiously Cat swallowed to ease her dry throat.

Nick said deliberately, 'So I decided that this was my chance to drive that hunger out once and for all. I thought I was being quite cold-blooded about it—I was prepared to use your need to help Juana to get you out of my system.' He straightened up, lean, graceful body stiff as he leaned back against the veranda support. 'I'm not proud of myself,' he said. 'It serves me right that it rebounded on me.'

Cat looked at him uncertainly. He was watching the children play in the rapidly thickening dusk. Another child, barely older, arrived at the gate and called with the arrogance of authority. Two of the playing children obeyed instantly, laughing as they ran towards her.

Cat said, 'Rebounded on you?'

Nick said, 'Moving you into my house made me realise that there was much more to you than a shallow-minded opportunist. In no time you had Mrs Hannay eating out of your hands, and Rob being fatherly—you even won Francesca over! And instead of dulling my need, I walked on red-hot wires, eaten up with it. You'd never have come to me yourself—you made that quite plain—but whenever you said my name I heard "I want you". So I made love to you, and you responded with a hot, earthy, generous passion that had me fighting a last rearguard action.'

She flushed. 'I must have been totally transparent.'

'I wouldn't say that.' His tone was wry, and still he didn't look at her, still kept his gaze fixed onto the children playing under the rain tree. 'After we'd made love, I looked at your sleeping face and knew that it wasn't enough. I wanted to hear "I love you" whenever you said my name.'

Cat's heart lurched, then sped up. She couldn't move, couldn't think.

'And that,' Nick said curtly, 'scared the hell out of me. I didn't want to love you.'

'Why?' she asked, still bewildered.

His jaw hardened and she saw him swallow. 'You're nothing like my mother, and by then I knew it, but it didn't stop me from making sure that—as you put it the next morning—you didn't get any ideas about your place in my life.'

Cat swung herself up onto the wide balustrade, tucked her knees under her chin and folded her arms around them. Like him, she kept her eyes on the children, grateful for the friendly dusk. 'It's not surprising that such a cruel, wicked abandonment marked you.'

'I didn't know that it had.' For the first time since the beginning of this odd, painful conversation he looked at her. Evening had pounced on the island, shadows creeping from the trees as the sun rushed headlong into the sea. In the dimness his face was all angles and planes, like a carving, emotionless and controlled. But his voice was quiet and completely sincere when he said, 'I'm sorry.'

'Nick, it's all right.'

He was silent for a moment. 'In the hospital you bent over Juana with tears in your eyes, and I finally understood that I was never going to get you out of my heart. It was like a bloody thunderclap. I love you, and I want you to love me. And immediately afterwards I realised that I had nothing to offer you, nothing you wanted from me except sex.'

And suddenly it was so easy. 'For a very clever man, you can be such an idiot sometimes,' she said adoringly, eyes flashing as she swung down and paced towards him. 'Didn't it ever occur to you that I might want *your* love?'

'It never occurred to me that my love was worth anything to you,' he returned, not moving.

She sensed the tension in him, and confidence rushed through her. 'Oh, Nick! I shouldn't blame you, because it's only while I stayed at your house that I realised I've loved you for years, ached for you, broken—'

Her words were lost as he kissed her, at first with a restrained passion.

But when Cat lifted herself up on tiptoes and opened her lips to him, the kiss deepened suddenly and dramatically. Eventually he tore his mouth away, groaning, 'Tell me to stop.'

'Why?' Her voice was husky and deliberate.

'Because I don't want to frighten you.'

She laughed huskily. 'Nothing you could do would scare me. Didn't I show you that when we made love? I think you've always thought of me as that eighteen-year-old girl you met first, who rejected you. I'm all grown up, Nick.' Her amusement turned to seriousness. Voice deepening, she finished, 'The only thing you could do to frighten me would be to leave me.'

'I'll never do that,' he promised against her mouth, making the words a vow.

Cat knew she should be happy, but she had to ask, 'Nick, what about Glen? Is he going to loom over us for the rest of our lives?'

'No,' he said quietly, his arms loosening around her. He looked down into her upturned face, his own uncompromising. 'I've come to terms with his memory. Wishing that I'd behaved differently, or that he had, is a waste of time and energy. He was flawed, but he gave me my chance.

While he was alive neither of us did anything to betray him, and you were a good wife to him. How do you feel?'

'I agree,' she said. 'When Morna told me how cruelly he'd treated her, I was able to be much more objective about him, see him not just as the man I married when I was in love with you—not as a victim.'

He said, 'He was sorry in the end. He left her enough money to set herself up; that's why she came back to New Zealand. I think when he realised he was going to die he finally understood what he'd done to her. And now, my dearest heart, she's been able to put him behind her. I don't know what you said to her—'

'Nothing. I just let her talk; I felt utterly futile!'

Nick laughed softly and gathered her closer. Against her cheek he said, 'Perhaps she just needed to let the poison out. Whatever, she's going to make it now. And so are we.'

A movement along the veranda swivelled them both around, and apart.

Apparently Sister Bernadette could see in the dark, because she said cheerfully, 'So you've settled your differences.'

'I think we have,' Nick said. 'Could we get married here, Sister?'

'In the eyes of God, certainly, although I don't know whether it will be legal in the eyes of man. You might have to go through another ceremony in New Zealand.'

Hot-cheeked, Cat laughed unsteadily at the nun's prompt reply. Nick's voice too showed that he was smiling. 'If it's not legal we can do it again in New Zealand, but I think Cat would like to be married here amongst her friends.'

He reached out and tucked Cat's hand into his. She leaned against him, lapped in the tenderness she had longed for.

'Very much,' she said, and the tropical night whispered headily around them all. 'Juana can be a flower girl,' she decided.

*   *   *

Decked out in her frilled and ruffled dress, carrying a little posy, Juana accompanied them to the altar in the makeshift church, gazing up with her wide, dark eyes as they were married. Rosita and the villagers had dressed Cat in island wedding clothes—scarlet and blue silk, with a diadem of scarlet and cream orchids, not caring a bit that the colours clashed with her hair.

Nick had produced the Tanzanite ring and the pearls, and wedding rings for them both, and there, with Stephanie and Adam Cowdray watching amidst the devout villagers, the priest married them.

'And the marriage is legal in New Zealand,' Nick told her afterwards, in a house on Fala'isi, a South Pacific island a thousand miles away from war-torn Romit. 'Not that it makes any difference—I've felt married to you since we made love. If I'd had any sense I'd have realised then that I loved you, and stopped fighting it.'

Cat gave him a hot, possessive look. 'Idiots, both of us,' she said languidly. 'Is this another of your houses?'

'No, it's Stan Barrington's, and that's a private beach,' Nick told her. 'We can stay here for as long as we like. According to Stan, Francesca is busy refusing to fall in love with a man who's making all the running. He thinks she might have met her match at last.'

'I'm so glad,' Cat said with a smile that held a tinge of relief. 'Darling, I do love you so much.'

He took her hand, and kissed the palm, and then each finger. 'And I love you,' he said deeply. 'So much more than I'll ever be able to tell you—always and for ever.'

The world's bestselling romance series.

HARLEQUIN®
Presents

Seduction and Passion Guaranteed!

Your dream ticket to the vacation of a lifetime!

Why not relax and allow Harlequin Presents® to whisk you away
to stunning international locations with our new miniseries...

*Where irresistible men and sophisticated women
surrender to seduction under the golden sun.*

Don't miss this opportunity to
experience glamorous lifestyles
and exotic settings in:

**Robyn Donald's
THE TEMPTRESS OF TARIKA BAY**
on sale July, #2336

**THE FRENCH COUNT'S MISTRESS
by Susan Stephens**
on sale August, #2342

**THE SPANIARD'S WOMAN
by Diana Hamilton**
on sale September, #2346

**THE ITALIAN MARRIAGE
by Kathryn Ross**
on sale October, #2353

FOREIGN AFFAIRS... A world full of passion!

**Pick up a Harlequin Presents® novel and you will enter a world
of spine-tingling passion and provocative, tantalizing romance!**

Available wherever Harlequin books are sold.

HARLEQUIN®
Live the emotion™

Visit us at www.eHarlequin.com   HPFAMA

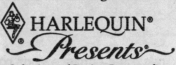

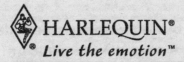

If you enjoyed what you just read,
then we've got an offer you can't resist!

Take 2 bestselling love stories FREE!

Plus get a FREE surprise gift!

The world's bestselling romance series.

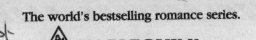

HARLEQUIN®
Presents

Seduction and Passion Guaranteed!

Back by popular demand...

trust but verified? (handwritten)

EXPECTING

*She's sexy,
successful
and
PREGNANT!*

Relax and enjoy our fabulous series about couples whose passion results in pregnancies...sometimes unexpected! Of course, the birth of a baby is always a joyful event, and we can guarantee that our characters will become besotted moms and dads—but what happened in those nine months before?

Share the surprises, emotions, drama and suspense as our parents-to-be come to terms with the prospect of bringing a new life into the world. All will discover that the business of making babies brings with it the most special love of all....

Our next arrival will be

PREGNANCY OF CONVENIENCE
by Sandra Field
On sale June, #2329

Pick up a Harlequin Presents® novel and you will enter a world of spine-tingling passion and provocative, tantalizing romance!

Available wherever Harlequin books are sold.

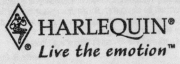

HARLEQUIN®
Live the emotion™

Visit us at www.eHarlequin.com   HPEXPJA